"Would you mind standing up and turning around?"

The earl's voice was deliberately benign.

Juliana knew well enough what to think of a man who would employ a governess based on physical attributes. She rose gracefully and turned on her heel without a word.

"Miss Chevron, wait! I have not finished—"

His presumption angered her. Juliana turned, eyes flashing. "How dare you, sir? I may be near destitute, but I am and shall always remain a *lady*."

"There was never a question of that, my dear girl. Had there been, you would not be considered for this position." He saw her hesitation and added, "I am offering a salary of one hundred pounds a year."

One hundred pounds! It was more than she could hope to earn in the next few years.

"Please be seated, Miss Chevron," the earl suggested gently.

"Thank you, my lord," Juliana responded reluctantly, adding, "but this does not mean I shall agree to accept your offer."

"You will, my dear. You will."

Books by Jeanne Carmichael

HARLEQUIN REGENCY ROMANCE
56—A TOUCH OF BLACKMAIL
67—QUEST FOR VENGEANCE

A MOMENT OF MADNESS

JEANNE CARMICHAEL

Harlequin Books

TORONTO • NEW YORK • LONDON
AMSTERDAM • PARIS • SYDNEY • HAMBURG
STOCKHOLM • ATHENS • TOKYO • MILAN
MADRID • WARSAW • BUDAPEST • AUCKLAND

For three very talented writers—
Deborah Barr, Ruth Owen and Cynthia Powell

Published June 1992

ISBN 0-373-31175-3

A MOMENT OF MADNESS

CHAPTER ONE

JULIANA CHEVRON straightened her back and gripped her reticule tighter as the butler indicated she should have a seat in the Great Hall. He told her, quite unnecessarily, that there were a number of applicants before her. She could see that for herself. There were a dozen older ladies in the Hall. She imagined all of them were better qualified, and wondered dismally if there were any point in waiting to see the earl.

Nevertheless, she thanked the man politely and seated herself carefully in a large wing chair. Juliana stared at the point above the doors, avoiding the looks of the other women, and prayed their prying eyes would not see the threadbare patches on the palms of her kid gloves.

Her stomach churned uneasily, reminding her that tea and toast was not a substantial breakfast. Anna had urged her to eat sensibly but she'd been too nervous. She desperately needed this position, and the notice in the *Gazette* had sounded so promising. She should have guessed that every impoverished lady in London would turn up at Cavendish Square.

The butler returned, and Juliana watched as he spoke quietly with an elderly woman before escorting her through the doors. She allowed herself to glance round the room then, and immediately wished she hadn't. The other ladies all looked so much older—and more competent. One woman, dressed appropriately in a drab brown pelisse, glared at her with obvious disdain.

She thinks I'm too young for such an important position, Juliana thought, and worried the earl would think so, too.

That was what Lady Poole had said when she'd dismissed her. Too young. Too pretty. Just because her impressionable son had fancied himself in love with the new governess. Poor Edward, Juliana thought as she recalled the lanky, awkward youth who had dogged her footsteps.

The door opened and her attention returned to the butler. He consulted a list and then gestured to the woman in the brown pelisse. She rose majestically, following the butler through the doors. She glanced back at Juliana, her face full of condescension. No need for you to remain now, her look seemed to say.

Juliana agreed. Only her dire need to find some kind of employment kept her from bolting. Anna had been so encouraging this morning, reminding her that the advertisement had been rather vague. Perhaps, Anna had said, the child in question would be quite young and her own youth would not be held against her. All the paper had stipulated was that the lady be of good breeding. Anna didn't see why anyone should object to having a pretty governess about, but Juliana knew the realities of earning a living. Youth and beauty were generally counted as liabilities.

Glancing down at her gown, Juliana frowned. She didn't look pretty now. She had taken pains to disguise her twenty-two years and her beauty. Anna had protested when Juliana insisted on wrapping her long, black hair tightly round her head, and worse, covering it up with one of her old bonnets. The faded blue day dress she wore had not met with her old nurse's approval, either. It was too big and hung in loose folds against Juliana's slender form.

"You can't be hiding your light beneath a bushel forever," Anna had said. Juliana wished she could. Her looks had caused her nothing but grief.

The butler appeared again, his double chins quivering as he called out the next name. Well, the lady in brown hadn't lasted long. She idly watched the next applicant trudge across the marble floor. An older woman, her shoulders stooped with age, wore a cloak of hopelessness about her that wrung a pang of sympathy from Juliana.

The woman looked as desperate as Juliana felt. She wondered if the old lady had a place to stay. At least she had Anna and her good-natured husband, William Goodbody, to provide her with a home. When she'd been dismissed from Lady Poole's, Juliana had called on her old nurse. Anna, of course, had insisted she stay with them until she found a new position.

She hated imposing on them. Their house, no more than a cottage really, was already overcrowded with their two boys. And for all Anna's protests, Juliana knew they could ill afford another mouth to feed. Still, there was little choice. Her entire savings consisted of three pounds. There was no place else she could go.

Juliana, her mind dwelling on her problems, was startled when the butler announced her name. She looked up in confusion.

"You're next, Miss. Come along."

She stood abruptly, almost tripping over the hem of her dress, and heard a titter from across the room. Juliana squared her shoulders and walked with as much dignity as she could muster, following the butler through the doors and down a long hall.

He paused, tapping briefly on a door before entering, and gestured impatiently for Juliana to follow him. "Miss Chevron, your lordship."

Spencer Drayton, the fourth Earl of Granville, stood behind an immense mahogany desk. Juliana's imagination took flight, and she fancied a long line of earls standing behind him. Each with the same regal bearing, wide shoulders and piercing eyes. He would have looked distinguished in a room full of princes and she knew an urge to flee.

"Come in, come in," he ordered briskly and watched critically as she crossed the room. He was inclined to dismiss her out of hand. He had specified a lady of impeccable breeding and what he was seeing were the dregs of society. This one looked no better than the others, and he waved impatiently to a pair of armchairs in front of the desk.

Juliana hesitantly took a seat, her hand gripping the gilt arm of the chair tightly. She glanced up, seeing only the man's stern face and unrelenting eyes. She had to swallow before she could speak.

"Thank you for seeing me, Lord Granville."

He didn't answer, too intent on studying her face and rapidly reconsidering his first estimate. This child could not be much above twenty. Moreover, she had green eyes like Lady Eastbourne, only a shade deeper and more heavily fringed. He liked the way her dark brows angled up above them.

"Would you mind removing your hat, Miss Chevron?"

Juliana lifted a hand hesitantly. "My bonnet? I don't quite understand."

"I like to see those I am dealing with. My father always said a man's face shows his character. I presume the same is true of ladies. Remove the bonnet, if you please."

Arrogant, she thought, and with nervous fingers untied the strings. She kept her eyes down as she lifted off the offending hat.

The earl's face showed nothing of the triumph he felt upon seeing the black hair. Luxuriant, rich-looking black hair like that of Lady Stapleton. So black it almost seemed a deep, luminous blue where the sunlight glinted on it.

Juliana, unnerved by his silence, looked up. It was impossible to tell what Lord Granville was thinking, but he did not appear approving. She felt a small measure of relief when he sat down. At least he was not dismissing her as fast as the lady in brown.

"Tell me, do you speak French? *Parlez-vous français?*"

"Bien sûr, monsieur," she answered and continued in flawless French, "My mother was an Englishwoman, but my papa was French and insisted I learn the language."

"Excellent," he said, but with such a lack of enthusiasm that he might have been commenting on the weather. Juliana fell silent and watched him.

He rested his elbows on the desk and brought his hands up, pressing the tips of his fingers together, considering her. She spoke the language as well as Lady Mary Montagu, and her voice had a low, melodious quality to it. Aunt Georgia would be delighted. He glanced down at his list of requirements and then back at Juliana. "You appear a well-educated and accomplished young woman. What other skills do you possess?''

''I play the harpsichord adequately, sketch a little and of course I was taught the intricacies of dance. I believe my skills are sufficient to teach, my lord.''

''And do you ride, Miss Chevron?''

Juliana's delicate brows lifted slightly. ''Would that be part of my duties?''

''Yes. My, er, charge is an avid horseman.''

''A little boy, then?'' She nodded, well pleased. Little boys were customarily provided better training than girls. ''I suppose I ride well enough, though it has been years since I've had the opportunity.''

The earl leaned back in his chair. ''Tell me something of your background, Miss Chevron. I believe you said your mother was English?''

''Yes, from the Isle of Wight. She met my father when he fled France after the Revolution.'' She paused, smiling. ''I understand it was love at first sight and they were wed within a matter of months.''

Granville sighed, his eyes involuntarily drawn to the portrait above the fireplace. He, too, had married for love. He contemplated the painting of a fashionable young woman in a blush-coloured gown for several minutes until a movement from Juliana recalled him.

''What of your mother's family? Did they object to the match?'' he asked more abruptly than he intended.

''My grandfather certainly did. He couldn't bear to see Mama wedding an impoverished émigré, and she had received two offers from other gentlemen he considered more suitable. But it was of little use. My mother was very determined and she declared she would have Christian Chevron or no one. Grandfather gave in at last, though he never really approved. He held it against her until—" She broke off, a shadow crossing her expressive eyes.

"Until?" the earl prompted.

"Until she died," Juliana finished in a rush. "My father had returned to France against all advice. He wished desperately to recover his estates. I fear my grandfather made living with him rather difficult. Papa never returned from that trip, and my mother grieved for him until she fell ill. She died a year later."

"I see. And your grandfather?"

"He raised me. I was ten at the time and remained with him until he died two years ago." The words were calmly spoken and she met his eyes directly.

"I do not wish to be impertinent, but did he make no provision for you?"

"He did the best he could, but he suffered severe losses himself. When he died, Carisbrook had to be sold to satisfy his creditors." She gave a typically Gallic shrug. "That is why I seek employment, my lord."

"Carisbrook? Are you General Claxton's granddaughter, then?"

Juliana nodded. "Did you know him?"

"He was a crony of my father's. We visited Carisbrook Hall when I was a boy. The old gentleman was something of a tartar, if I recollect correctly."

"You do, sir," she replied, laughing at that mild description of her grandfather's tyrannical disposition.

The earl nodded his approval. When she laughed like that, it lit her eyes and curved her cheekbones. Not only did she have the requisite breeding, but he suspected she was a beauty. Now for the final test. It was difficult to judge her figure beneath that awful dress, but necessary. John was a connoisseur. He stood. "Would you mind standing up and turning round?"

Juliana remained seated, the laughter dying in her eyes. She knew well enough what to think of a man who would employ a governess based on physical attributes. How foolish she'd been to allow herself to hope she'd found a good position. Her disappointment washed over her, eroding her strength.

"Miss Chevron—" the earl prodded, walking round the desk.

Juliana exerted her will over her weary body and rose gracefully. Her green eyes raked over him, conveying the full measure of her contempt. She turned on her heel without a word.

"Miss Chevron, wait! I have not finished—"

His presumption angered her. Juliana turned, eyes flashing and her slender body trembling visibly beneath the shabby dress. "How dare you, sir? I may be near destitute, but I am and shall remain a *lady*."

"There was never a question of that, my dear girl. Had there been, you would not be considered for this position."

His voice, his bearing and the look in his pale blue eyes told her the earl was offended. Confused, Juliana hesitated.

"I suggest you return to your chair and we discuss this like rational beings—that is, if you are interested in the position." He saw her hesitation and added, "I am offering a salary of one hundred pounds a year."

One hundred pounds! It was more than she had earned in two years. More than she could hope to earn in the next few years. With a hundred pounds she could even afford to help Anna and Will. She relented, walking slowly towards him. He was not as tall as she had first supposed, and her eyes were on a level with his chin. A square-cut, domineering chin with a cleft just below the full lower lip. She raised her eyes to his and saw a kindness reflected there, which unsettled her more than his arrogance.

"Please be seated, Miss Chevron."

"Thank you, my lord, but before we continue, I should like to know the exact nature of this position."

"Certainly." He held the chair for her, and when she was comfortably seated, returned to his own. He had seen enough, and pulled the bell rope behind the desk. "I have a proposition to put before you." He held up a hand as she opened her mouth to protest. "A perfectly innocent offer, I assure you."

Juliana thought she saw a flash of humour in his pale eyes, but it was gone in an instant.

"One moment," he said, looking expectantly towards the door. His butler appeared as if on cue and bowed. Lord Granville requested tea be served. The man nodded, his heavy jowls shaking, and turned to go when the earl added, "And, Hadley, please thank all the other applicants and send them away."

Juliana said nothing until the doors closed behind the butler. "Are you not being precipitate, my lord?"

"I think not. I have interviewed above a score of ladies, none of whom came even remotely close to meeting my requirements. That is, until your arrival. I believe we shall deal admirably together." His long, elegant fingers toyed with the pen on his desk and Juliana felt he was toying with her, as well.

"I trust your confidence will not be misplaced, sir, but I cannot agree until I know the terms of employment. How old is the boy?"

"We will discuss the *boy* over tea," he said with a half smile.

The odd emphasis he placed on the word left her feeling uneasy, but Hadley returned with the tea tray before she could comment. The earl directed him to place the service on a mahogany table near the fireplace, and then came round the desk to offer his arm. "Shall we, Miss Chevron?"

Juliana allowed him to lead her to a low serpentine settee facing the table and flanked by two matching armchairs. She was relieved when he took one of the chairs, but the relentless assessment of his eyes made her uncomfortable. She glanced round the elegant room, searching for a polite topic of conversation.

"Would you pour out, my dear? All this interviewing has left my throat quite parched."

Juliana removed her gloves and carefully placed them on her bonnet beside her. With all the grace she could command, she poured the tea and passed a delicate china cup to the earl, feeling all the while as if she were under the most intense scrutiny.

"This is a most unusual table, my lord," she said, hoping she managed to sound assured. The tabletop had a leather centre surrounded by a wide gilt metal rim. The rim itself was inset with twelve rectangular ivory miniatures, depicting various scenes from mythology.

"Your taste is exceptional. Of all the objects in this room, that table is perhaps the most valuable."

"I doubt it requires good taste to admire a work of art, my lord."

"No, only to recognize it. As you can see, I have resisted the urge to adorn the room with crocodile legs and sphinx heads."

His reference to the current decorating rage relaxed Juliana enough to smile. Well-shaped lips parted over tiny white teeth and her green eyes took on an added warmth. "It would not suit you nearly so well," she said without thinking.

"Perhaps not, but there are those who find this room sadly lacking." He did not quite smile at her, but his tone conveyed his approval.

Juliana wondered how he would look if he ever laughed, and then abruptly recalled her situation. "I believe you were about to tell me how old the boy is."

"The boy? Oh, yes. My younger brother is seven-and-twenty, Miss Chevron."

She stared at him. Was he jesting? If so, she was not amused. She held her tongue and waited for him to explain.

"Have you perhaps heard of Lord John Drayton?" he asked, setting down his cup and leaning forward.

"Madcap Johnny, do you mean? I doubt there is anyone in all England who has not heard that name."

"Unfortunately, I fear you are correct. Lord John is my younger brother."

Juliana was astonished. Madcap Johnny, the beloved darling of the ton, the dashing, handsome nonpareil, related to this man? She could not believe it. Not knowing what to say, she took refuge in sipping her tea.

The earl watched her, wondering how to phrase his outrageous proposition. Deciding directness would serve him best, he asked abruptly, "Would you consider wedding such a man?"

Juliana choked over her tea and hastily put her cup down. "Really, Lord Granville, I fail to see what all this has to do with my employment."

"Answer me, please."

His voice was compelling and Juliana shrugged. It could not hurt to humour the man. "I doubt I ever would have such an opportunity, my lord. We hardly move in the same circles. But yes, I suppose I would consider it. I have heard he is most handsome, charming and the Catch of the Season."

"He is also extremely reckless, irresponsible, a spendthrift and a profligate. He would not be a bargain as a husband, Miss Chevron."

Juliana refilled his cup, a smile lingering on her lips. "Much is forgiven a gentleman of pleasing countenance and charming manners, sir. But as I said, I doubt I would ever have the opportunity, so it is hardly my concern."

Lord Granville stood and, taking a few steps, came to stand behind her. His hands rested on the curved back of the settee, and his voice floated down over her shoulder. "Lord John is my heir. It is my desire that he wed and set up his nursery. I have given this a great deal of thought and I believe he can be persuaded to do so provided I can find a lady who meets all his requirements."

Juliana's hands trembled as an outlandish notion entered her head. She carefully sat her cup on the tray and turned to look up at the earl. The vague wording of the advertisement in the *Gazette* came back to her. "An accomplished lady of impeccable breeding needed for a position in the Earl of Granville's home." No. It was preposterous.

The earl saw her understanding and nodded. "You meet all the requirements, Miss Chevron."

"You are insane, my lord! You cannot mean to find a wife for your brother by advertising in the paper. It's absurd, inconceivable."

"I thought so at first," he said, returning to his chair, and stretching out his long legs. "When my Aunt Georgia proposed the idea, I was aghast. However, on consideration, I found it to have some merit, and John's latest exploit has convinced me that something must be done immediately."

Juliana shook her head. "I cannot give credence to your words, sir. Surely this is some manner of jest?"

"I promise you I am quite serious."

"But your brother? You cannot expect him to agree to such a scheme? What will you do? Have him drop by and introduce him to me? 'Look, John, I have found a wife for you. I advertised in the *Gazette* and Miss Chevron appeared on my doorstep.'"

"No, my dear, I am not so vulgar as that, nor so foolish."

Juliana gathered her gloves and her bonnet and rose. "Forgive my plain speaking, my lord, but you are indeed foolish—foolish beyond belief."

"Sit down, Miss Chevron. At least, finish your tea while I explain. When you are done, if I have not persuaded you, I shall send you home in my carriage and recompense you for your time."

Juliana looked at him helplessly.

"Please," he added.

It would be churlish of her to refuse, and certainly it would do her no harm merely to listen, Juliana reasoned, seating herself once again.

Lord Granville sat opposite, and this time it was he who poured out the tea. He passed a cup to Juliana and then, while adding sugar to his own, began to speak.

"We have a common bond, Miss Chevron. I, too, lost my parents at a tender age. I was fourteen when my father died, and John only eight."

Juliana sipped her tea, rapidly calculating. The earl then must be three-and-thirty. Odd, she had thought him considerably older. Perhaps it was the silver-grey at his temples which made him appear so mature, or perhaps his air of elegance and sophistication. Young gentlemen never seemed to achieve that level of confidence. Juliana realized her wits were wandering and brought her attention back to the earl.

"We had the requisite nanny and tutors, of course," he was saying, "but I considered myself responsible for John. When he was younger, I found his escapades engaging, and no doubt I unwittingly cheered him on. He was such a brave little devil and without an ounce of fear in him."

A tinge of admiration coloured his voice and Juliana warmed towards him. "You were fortunate to have a brother, sir. I was an only child."

"It is not always a blessing, I assure you. Especially not the past few years. John's exploits have grown wilder and his name has been linked with one scandal after another. The ladies seem to find him all too charming and overly encourage him." He paused, looking at her, a gleam of speculation in his eyes. "I hope that with my help, you will put an end to such behaviour."

"Even were I so obliging, my lord, you would set me an impossible task. How could I hope to succeed where so many others have failed? Gossip has it that every eligible miss in London has thrown her cap at Mad—at Lord John."

"Ah, but *you* would have my help. I know his every like and dislike and have prepared a list of those traits he most admires. I could groom you to be irresistible in his eyes."

Juliana laughed aloud, and set down her cup. "You are too absurd, my lord. One cannot legislate the more tender emotions."

"I disagree, Miss Chevron, and am willing to make it worth your time if you will indulge me in this. I promise you, even if I am proved wrong, you will not fail to benefit."

"How may that be, sir?" she asked, more out of curiosity than any desire to participate in so mad a scheme.

"If you agree to my terms, you will remove at once to Crowley, my country seat in Chelmsford. There you will be completely outfitted by the finest modiste in London. My aunt and I shall teach you John's likes and dislikes and you will become proficient in those skills my brother most admires. When we deem you ready, you will be presented to the ton as a protégée of my aunt's. You will move in the first circles, Miss Chevron, and if my plan succeeds, you will become Lady Drayton, and ultimately, the Countess of Granville."

"And if your plan fails?" she asked, thinking the idea absurd.

"You will still have your salary, your wardrobe, and I and my aunt will do everything possible to find you a good position."

Juliana sat back, shaking her head. "I cannot credit this madness, but for the sake of argument, suppose I did agree. Suppose I am groomed and presented. Your brother falls wildly in love and makes me an offer."

The earl was almost smiling, nodding his head in encouragement.

Juliana's green eyes danced with amusement as she peered at him over the rim of her cup. "And then, I find that after all I cannot accept this madcap brother of yours."

"Hardly a likelihood," the earl murmured, relieved she had not placed some obstacle in his way. "I have yet to encounter a young lady immune to his charm. *That* is part of my problem. But if, as you say for the sake of argument, you feel you must draw back, then our bargain still stands."

"You are willing to risk a great deal merely to see your brother wed."

"I am," he said, lifting his chin with pride. "He is my heir, the last of the Draytons. I wish the line to continue."

"Then why not wed yourself?"

Her remark was an impertinence and he regarded her with cool eyes, but owned that under the circumstances it was a fair question. "I did wed. My wife died only eight months after our marriage. She was the perfect lady—nearly a saint. I still cherish her memory and have no desire to ever set another in her place."

Juliana, about to say poppycock, bit her tongue and looked away. When she brought her eyes back to the earl, he appeared lost in thought. She should not have been surprised that a man capable of dreaming up such an improbable scheme would harbour such idiotish sentiments. To her practical mind, love matches were nonsensical. She knew firsthand what misery awaited a misalliance.

Granville turned towards her, making an effort to smile. "Well, Miss Chevron, what say you? Have we a bargain?"

Her eyes met his. Of course he was insane, but the offer was tempting. One hundred pounds was a small fortune. She could stock the larder for Anna, afford to buy Will a new dray and boots for both the boys. She glanced down at her threadbare gloves. It was certainly tempting. "I will consider your offer, my lord, on one condition."

"Yes?"

"You say this...idea was your aunt's and it is she who will sponsor me?" He nodded, and she continued, "Then I should first like to meet this lady."

"Capital!" he said, rising. "I will send my carriage for you tomorrow afternoon and we shall join her for tea."

His enthusiasm was too marked and she cautioned, "I have not yet agreed to your offer, Lord Granville."

"Haven't you, my dear?"

CHAPTER TWO

"I STILL DON'T LIKE IT, Miss Juliana. It's not fitting behaviour for a young lady. What manner of man can this Madcap Johnny be if his own brother must deceive him?" Anna Goodbody punched the dough she was kneading, adding emphasis to her words and scattering flour across the table.

Juliana, her chair well out of harm's way, smiled at her old nurse. "He's the sort every lady in London wishes she could wed. He's handsome, charming—"

"And a care-for-nobody. You know I don't hold none with gossip but where there's smoke, there's likely fire, and if only half the things I've heard be true, he ain't the sort of gentleman your mama would be wanting you to marry." She paused, wiping the sweat from her brow, the flour cascading down her face and across her ample bosom.

"I do not *have* to marry him, Anna. Lord Granville made that clear." Juliana rose and crossed to the window, looking out into the small yard. William was out there loading a cumbersome cart. Tommy, the older boy, was helping him manoeuvre the heavy pieces of furniture and young Willie was, as usual, getting underfoot. She saw the boy toss a stick for the outsize mongrel pup he insisted on calling Cyclops, and smiled as the animal took a shortcut between Tommy's legs to fetch it. The yard was busy this morning, but there was no sign of the earl's carriage.

"Him! He's no better 'an that brother of his, if you was to ask me. Thinking up such a ramshackle affair and dragging you into it." Anna turned the dough and plunked it down with enough force to send the orange tabby scurrying from beneath the table, taking refuge against Juliana's boots. "Stay away from that cat or he'll have hair all over you. If you insist on taking tea with *that* woman—"

"Lady Alynwick," Juliana supplied, stooping to scratch the tabby's head.

"*That* woman," Anna continued. "Leastways you can go looking like a proper lady. Go on, Mouser, scat!"

The cat fled to the relative safety of the sitting room, and Juliana obediently shook out the folds of her jonquil walking dress.

Anna stood still, watching her, a suspicious moisture in her eyes. "You look more like your mama every day. I can't think what she be saying if she knew the pass you've come to. 'Tis shameful." She shook her head, using the corner of her dusty apron to dab at her eyes.

"Anna, please don't. The earl seems like a most respectable gentleman, truly he does." She took a step towards her old nurse, intent on offering what comfort she could, but Anna backed away.

"Don't be hugging me now, child. You'll be getting flour all over you and then what would your fine earl say?"

"Why, that I must love you very dearly. Anna, I cannot bear seeing you looking so sad."

"Go on with you. You'll not be getting by me with your smiles and hugs." The tone was rough but a glimmer of a smile lurked at her mouth as she picked up her dough, and then paused, tilting her head.

They both heard the sound of a carriage and team and Juliana hurried to the window. An elegant equipage with a crested door panel, drawn by four matching chestnuts, was pulling into the drive next to the dray. It could only belong to the earl. William did not receive such carriages in his yard.

"He's here," red-headed Willie yelled, barrelling through the kitchen door. "It's the biggest coach I ever seen and four bang-up ones a-pulling it," he panted, and duty done, rushed out again.

"Mind the cat," Anna warned, an instant too late. The orange tabby saw his chance and streaked through the kitchen, eluding Juliana's hands, and bolting for freedom. "Drat that animal," Anna moaned, trotting after him.

Mouser had already seen the danger and didn't need the excited yapping of the mongrel pup to alert him. He barely broke stride as he leaped onto the heavy settee William and Tommy were balancing between them, and from there to the top of the dray.

William stumbled, but he was a strong, brawny man and would have recovered if Cyclops hadn't followed suit. The weight of the dog was too much. He went down in a heap, narrowly missing a large puddle, and as the settee tilted, Cyclops tumbled on top of him. William lay on the ground, mildly cursing, and smacked the animal soundly. The dog scrambled off with a yelp and chased round the cart to get at Mouser from the other side. Willie ran after him, loudly commanding him to heel, but the mutt had no manners. He lunged at the cart, yapping all the time, while Mouser perched precariously only inches above him.

A few feet away, the steps were let down and the Earl of Granville descended from his carriage and into bedlam. Mouser, no doubt seeing the earl's tall form as a safer post, leaped. Claws came out, digging into the earl's shoulder and tearing down the back of his elegant coat. Cyclops, giving chase, barked once and then bounded against the earl's chest, knocking him to the muddy ground.

The orange tabby beat a retreat round the cart, over the upturned settee and back to the house. Anna, watching aghast from the open door, saw him streak by. She stepped outside, shutting the door firmly in front of Cyclops. The mongrel gave a last bark of satisfaction, pleased to have rid the yard of the beast, and lay at her feet, his tail thumping.

Willie, red hair hanging in his face and dirt stains down his shirt, stared at the earl, his brown eyes round with awe at the destruction his pup had wrought. "Cor!"

Anna, with William and Tommy on her heels, hurried to assist the driver easing Lord Granville to his feet. She grabbed his right arm as he struggled up, murmuring apologies and praying the gentleman had come to no harm. When he stepped back, she was appalled to see her handprints on the damp sleeve of his lordship's blue coat.

"What the devil do you mean allowing that animal to run wild? He should be kept chained!" Granville declared, tugging at his waistcoat and brushing futilely at his sleeves.

"I'm right sorry, my lord," Anna began, but was cut off by Willie's protest.

"Cyclops's a good dog. He don't mean you no harm. It was Ma's cat that started the ruckus."

Anna grabbed him by the ear. "That'll be enough out of you. Say you're sorry to his lordship and then put that miserable mutt in the stable where he belongs."

Willie hung his head and mumbled something which might have passed as an apology. His pa cuffed him on the shoulder, named him a worthless lout and sent him stumbling towards the house.

William turned to the earl, hastily removing his cap and twisting it between his strong hands. "I be William Goodbody, my lord. If you come for Miss Juliana, I hope you won't be holding this mishap against her. She's a good girl, sir, and deserving better 'an what she's got."

"Mr. Goodbody," the earl acknowledged. "I do not wish to appear rude, but I find I have little desire to linger here. If Miss Chevron is ready, please inform her that the carriage is waiting."

"She's in the house, my lord," Anna said. "Will you step in, sir? While she fetches her gloves and bonnet, I could brush your coat off a mite."

The earl, doubting a brushing would do his ruined coat much good, agreed reluctantly. He followed her, bending his head beneath the low frame of the kitchen door. Anna would have taken him to the front, proper like, but it would have meant trudging through the mud puddles in the yard, and his lordship's glossy boots were already sadly splattered.

Juliana, who had watched the entire fiasco from the window, struggled to hide her laughter as the earl entered the kitchen. His cravat, once snow-white silk, was askew and splotched with dirt. The fine blue kerseymere coat, now soiled and damp, looked as though Cyclops had walked on it. Buff pantaloons had taken the worst of the muddy rainwater, and his boots would surely bring tears to his valet's eyes. It was a far cry from the immaculate gentleman who had peered down his aristocratic nose at her yesterday.

The earl, catching sight of her, read her thoughts easily. It was all he needed to complete his humiliation. "Go ahead and laugh, Miss Chevron. I fancy the boot is on the other foot today."

Her eyes danced but she only smiled. "I could not be so unkind, sir. My mama always said a true lady never seeks to make another feel uncomfortable."

"Then pray remove that cat before he mistakes me yet again for a safe perch!" the earl entreated, with a wary eye on Mouser resting atop a stand of cabinets.

"Oh, you need have no fear now, my lord. Mouser is really very well behaved. It is only since Willie brought Cyclops home—"

"Cyclops? He named that infernal mongrel Cyclops? How appropriate, for a more slovenly, ill-mannered beast I never saw." He turned slightly as Anna sponged the stains on his jacket.

"I fear you are in the right of it, but Willie was more taken with the tale of how the Cyclops slaughtered and then devoured any strangers approaching their shores. He means the mongrel to be a watchdog."

The earl, leaving his uncharitable opinion of the animal's potential for such a thing unvoiced, directed his attention to Mrs. Goodbody. "Thank you, madam, but that is sufficient. If Miss Chevron is ready, we must take our leave. My aunt is expecting us."

"Just let me brush the side here, my lord," Anna said, turning him slightly and vigorously applying her brush.

"Oh, gracious!" Juliana cried as she saw the strips of cloth hanging in tatters from the back of the earl's jacket. "I had no notion the cat clawed you so badly. Are you hurt, sir?"

The earl, glancing over his shoulder at the damage, looked up to meet her eyes with something akin to humour. "Only my pride, Miss Chevron."

Willie came in then, his scrawny frame dirtier than ever. He shuffled his feet, begging pardon and asked leave to speak to his lordship.

That he had been properly chastened, the earl had no doubt. The boy's brown eyes were red at the rims and his freckled cheeks were streaked from tears. The woebegone face reminded him of Johnny when he was a lad and in a scrape. He spoke more gently than might have been expected. "Willie, is it? Have you tied up your ferocious beast?"

"He's in the stable, sir," the boy assured him in an agony of embarrassment. "He didn't mean to go and knock you down, ruining your coat and all. I saved up three pence, sir. You could maybe have it mended." He held out a grubby hand with his hard-earned pennies.

The earl took the pennies, and with a solemn face, thanked him.

"Pa says, you being an earl and all, you could have Cyclops shot for jumping on you."

"I think your pa rather overestimates my powers, Willie. The animal should make a fine guard dog if you will only train him properly."

The boy nodded eagerly. "He's just a pup, yet, but I already learnt him to fetch. I've been trying to teach 'im to heel, but he runs off every time he sees a—"

"A cat? Well, that's the natural order of things. I'll tell you what—I have a man who works for me who has a way with dogs. He's trained several of mine. If you like, I could send him round. Perhaps he could give you a pointer or two."

When they left the cottage a few minutes later, Juliana was much in charity with the earl. His adroit handling of Willie pleased her. Another gentleman might have laughed at the lad's earnest effort to make amends, but Granville had taken the pence, salvaging the boy's pride. And the offer of help to train the animal had Willie in high gig. Even Anna had approved, whispering to Juliana as she left that perhaps the man was not as bad as she'd feared.

The warm feeling didn't last. The earl did not utter a word during the brief carriage drive to Grosvenor Square, and the moment they were admitted to Lady Alynwick's, he reverted to the dignified persona of an elder statesman. A ludicrous position to take in view of his dishevelled appearance.

Lady Alynwick's butler, a tall cadaverous fellow, looked down his long, pinched nose and was hard put not to show his astonishment. It was well for Granville that the man had not glimpsed the back of the earl's coat, hanging in tatters. Juliana had thought the earl high in the instep, but he hadn't a patch on the butler, whose haughty disdain was all too evident.

They were shown into a small, crimson drawing-room and asked to wait. It seemed Lady Alynwick was entertaining other visitors. Granville, conducting himself as though at home, strode at once to a black, japanned sideboard and poured himself a liberal drink from a crystal decanter. He caught sight of Juliana in the gilded wall mirror and waited to see her reaction to the room.

Juliana was fascinated. The furniture was all heavy black lacquer with elaborate gold designs and splashes of vivid crimson or scarlet. Three walls were covered with detailed Chinese wallpaper panels forming a continuous scene of pagodas before a lake, with huge mountains towering in the background. The fourth wall was broken by a bank of windows, draped in crimson velvet and tied back with elaborate gold tassels. She stepped closer to examine a sofa done in red, blue and green needlepoint against a black background. The Chinese pattern was repeated in the matching armchairs and two walnut footstools.

"The effect is rather overwhelming, is it not?" the earl asked, coming to join her.

"I have never seen anything so...so exotic," Juliana said, continuing to gaze at the unique furnishings. "But what a delightful room to spend a rainy afternoon in."

"Thank you, my dear."

Juliana spun round as Lady Alynwick swept into the room. She was tiny, barely five foot, and elegantly gowned in a willow-green dress which complemented her ivory complexion, blond hair and blue eyes.

"I am pleased you found us someone with exceptional taste, Spencer," Lady Alynwick said, offering him her cheek. She accepted his chaste salute, wrinkling her tiny nose. "Really, darling, you smell of the stable, and before you criticize my taste I suggest you look in the mirror." She gave him no opportunity to answer, turning to survey Juliana. "You must be Miss Chevron. Spencer scarcely did you credit."

"Miss Chevron, may I present my aunt, Lady Alynwick?" the earl said, with a long-suffering sigh.

"Amelia Eastbourne will be quite cast in the shade," the diminutive blonde declared, ignoring him. "Which is just as well, for I never fancied having her in the family." She gestured with her fan for Juliana to join her on the sofa. The earl, not waiting for an invitation, took the facing armchair.

"Now, my dear child, we have no time to waste. I have Princess Esterhazy and Maria Sefton calling shortly, and there's no putting them off. If Spencer had only told me sooner—well, no sense in crying over spilt milk, and I don't mean to reproach him. I am sure he managed as best he could. Grim will bring in our tea, and then we shall talk."

Juliana, feeling as though she were engulfed by a whirlwind, looked helplessly at the earl. He was of no help, intent on arguing with his aunt.

"I wish you would cease calling Hornsby by that ridiculous name."

"Nonsense. He quite likes it. Oh, there you are, Grim. Just in time, thank you."

The gaunt butler, his pale face expressionless, held the door open for a trim serving girl. He watched her carefully as she settled a heavy tray on the table before Lady Alynwick, and then ushered her from the room, pausing at the door. "Will there be anything else, my lady?"

"Nothing, thank you, Grim."

"Thank you, Hornsby," the earl said, and at Juliana's look of bewilderment, explained. "Aunt Georgia insists on calling the fellow Grim because she feels

Hornsby doesn't suit him. I warn you, Miss Chevron, changing names is a habit of hers and you shall likely find yourself rechristened."

"Do not be petulant, Spencer. Juliana Chevron is a lovely name and I see no reason to alter it." She leaned forward and patted Juliana's hand. "Do you take cream, my dear?"

"Yes, please," she replied with a laugh, accepting the proffered cup. Whatever else the position might offer, it promised to be amusing if Lady Alynwick had charge of it. She might be years older than the earl, but she had twice his energy and an air of infectious gaiety.

"Now, then, Miss Chevron—no, I cannot call you that."

"I warned you," Granville said, with what might have passed for a smile.

"Spencer, do behave. I only meant that Miss Chevron is too formal. After all, if she is to be part of the family, we must not stand on ceremony. I shall call you Juliana, and you must call me Georgia, if that is agreeable?"

"She has not yet accepted the position, Aunt."

"No? Then you have not explained it properly." She turned to Juliana. "My dear girl, what has he said to put you off? Come now, you may be frank with me."

"It is nothing Lord Granville said...I just never considered taking such a position. Forgive me, Lady Alynwick, but the entire notion seems insane."

"Indeed? We must talk then, but first—" She broke off, gesturing to Granville. "I do not mean to be unkind, and you know I adore you, but I *cannot* abide that appalling odour another minute. I am sure you have ample time to drive home and change while I chat with Juliana."

Her nephew rose with lazy grace and stooped to place a kiss on top of the blond curls. "Slyboots. Your Machiavellian instincts would put Bonaparte to shame." He bowed to Juliana. "I warn you, Miss Chevron, you are in the hands of a master strategist. Some of the best marriages in the ton are the result of my aunt's contrivance."

Juliana looked a shade apprehensive as he strolled from the room, and Georgia Alynwick smiled ruefully.

"It's quite true, my dear. I cannot seem to keep from meddling—it adds spice to my life. Now, do not look alarmed. My little intrigues are always for the best. The only time I ever failed was with Spencer."

"Lord Granville? But he said his wife was perfect. I had the impression he still mourns her."

"He does, and nothing could be more unfortunate," Georgia said, settling back more comfortably. She used her hands expressively as she talked, the flash of diamonds and rubies seeming to punctuate her words. "Cynthia March was a nice enough girl, I suppose, though she was not my choice for Spencer."

Juliana smiled knowingly.

"No, don't think I held that against her. She was very young, just out of the schoolroom and quite lovely but without an ounce of spirit to her. Her papa was a vicar, and not just one of those who give lip-service to their living. He was a real believer and he raised his daughter all prim and proper. Surely you know the sort?"

"The sort who would certainly frown upon the mad scheme you and Lord Granville propose," Juliana suggested with a deliberately solemn face.

"Precisely." Georgia nodded, undaunted. "I am glad to see you have a lively mind. You will have need of it with Johnny. Dear Cynthia never approved of Johnny. In point of fact, I don't believe she approved of Spencer, either, though she was glad enough to marry him. She set about changing him before they were even wed. He mustn't laugh so loud, he mustn't waltz, he mustn't have more than a glass of sherry." She shook her blond curls. "The list was endless and only a saint could have pleased her."

Juliana knew she should not be indulging in such a conversation. This was highly personal and Lord Granville would certainly not approve. When she had dared to ask about his wife, he had cut her off, his voice icy enough to freeze the Thames. But she was not as virtuous as Cynthia, and curiosity won out. "He must have loved her very much to have accepted such censure. He strikes me as being most proud."

Georgia nodded. "That's Cynthia's doing. She was forever reminding him of his consequence. Poor boy, he was infatuated by a pretty face and never looked beyond it. Had she lived, she would have driven him mad. I think the blush was already off the rose when she died. Spencer was spending more time in London and leaving dear Cynthia in the country. He was addressing the House when she died. It was a senseless accident, and no one could possibly be held to blame, but Spencer carries the guilt like sackcloth and ashes."

"I don't understand. If no one was to blame—"

"He blames himself, child. If he had been the saint Cynthia wanted, and to Spencer's mind, deserved, then he would have been with her. Might have prevented the accident. It's all nonsense, of course. Cynthia approved of his work in Parliament, and urged him to speak on all manner of causes. But I think Spencer used it as an excuse to escape from her. He's too much the gentleman to ever say anything, but I saw how it was. Saw the change in him and I knew there was trouble between them. It was a bad match. The chit should have married a missionary, or someone like Johnny who would have laughed at her strictures. Now, mind you, not a word to Spencer about this. I would not have mentioned it, but it's as well you know if you're going to be part of the family."

Juliana sat her cup down carefully. "Lady Alynwick, I—"

"You must call me Georgia, dear girl."

"Thank you, but I don't see how this…this plan of yours can possibly succeed. And while I don't wish to sound like Cynthia, it seems almost immoral to be scheming to entrap Lord John."

Whatever reaction Juliana expected, it was not the delicate trill of laughter she heard.

Lady Alynwick leaned forward and clasped her hand. "Dear girl, pray tell me you are not so naive. Why, if ladies did not scheme to entrap their gentlemen, there would be no marriages! What else is courtship? Why else do young ladies parade their wares at Almack's?"

"It's not quite the same thing," Juliana protested, at a loss to explain the difference.

"No? A young lady wears her prettiest gown and tortures her hair into the most attractive style. And for what? The admiration of other ladies? No, my child. It is all to entrap a gentleman."

"But what you are suggesting… You are conniving against your nephew. It seems rather unfair."

"It's for his own good," Georgia said firmly. "And after all, we cannot force him to offer for you."

Juliana was not certain of that and her green eyes revealed her scepticism perfectly.

"I am very fond of Johnny. I only wish to see him wed before some woman brings him to a disgraceful end. Now, is that such a bad thing?" she asked, contriving to look both hurt and innocent.

"No, of course not, and if you merely introduced him to some suitable young ladies, it would be nothing out of the ordinary. But to advertise for such a person..." The laughter in Georgia's eyes stopped her and her own lips curved into a smile as she added the ultimate condemnation. "*Dear Cynthia* would not approve of this, you must know."

Georgia hugged her. "When Spencer told me about you, I knew I would adore you. Now, be a darling girl and pour us a fresh cup of tea while I fetch my lists. I won't be above a moment," Georgia promised, disappearing in a swirl of green silk.

Juliana did as she'd been bade and, taking a reviving sip of the hot tea, wondered at her capitulation. Lady Alynwick was indeed a formidable strategist. If it had been left to Granville to persuade her, she doubted she would have agreed to such an outrageous and impossible scheme—even given the enormous salary he offered. She thought again of the hundred pounds and how much good she could do with it.

Juliana sat musing over what she might purchase first, until an alluring whiff of gardenias heralded Lady Alynwick's return.

"Here you are, darling girl," she said, thrusting a sheaf of papers in Juliana's lap as she sat down. "I am astonished at how closely you resemble Johnny's ideal lady. Only look at that list.''

Juliana scanned the delicately penned lines and then read aloud, ''Item one, hair as black as Lady Stapleton's.''

''Johnny vastly admires the lady's hair, but Maria does not have such a shine to hers. Does yours curl naturally?'' At Juliana's nod, she smiled. ''I thought so. Maria has to tie hers in paper and she uses false pieces a great deal of the time. Of course, gentlemen never notice those details, at least not until after the wedding.''

''Item two, green eyes like Lady Eastbourne's.''

''Yours are quite beautiful, child, and there is no need to blush. A woman does well to recognize her assets.''

''Item three—'' Juliana paused, the blush in her cheeks deepening. She was thankful Lord Granville was not present.

''A figure to rival that of Elizabeth Gresham,'' Georgia supplied, nodding her head. ''Spencer said he was not quite certain, but I think, once we have you properly gowned, Miss Gresham will have cause to worry.''

Juliana, her face burning, silently read the rest of the list. She must be able to dance gracefully, play the harpsichord skilfully, speak French fluently, converse with humour and wit and drive a team. That was only the beginning. Another page detailed the colours Lord John preferred, a second sheet listed his favourite foods, another the plays he most enjoyed and a fourth contained the music he most admired.

Lady Alynwick was nothing if not thorough, Juliana thought. It did appear she had much in common with Lord John, but there were two items on the list which disturbed her.

"I have never driven a team," she said, looking up at Georgia. "There is little hope I could ever compete with Diana Fielding. It's been years since I even sat a horse." The Fielding was notorious for driving a high-perch phaeton through the Park.

"You need not become a whipster," Georgia assured her. "Spencer will teach you to handle a team credibly. He is a member of the Four-in-Hand Club. Don't frown, Juliana. It wrinkles the skin. I promise you, you may rely on Spencer."

"For what, if I may be permitted to ask?" Lord Granville stood in the doorway, impeccably groomed.

"Hello, darling. You look much improved," Georgia said, waving a hand. "We were just discussing Diana Fielding. Juliana doesn't drive."

The earl glanced at her. "Have you decided, then?"

Juliana looked away. Granville had seemed almost human in his tattered coat and stained pantaloons. He had shed that image with his discarded clothing. Dressed conservatively in a bottle-green coat, he seemed distant, almost angry.

"Of course she has, darling. Don't be tiresome," Georgia answered him. "What has happened to disturb you, Spencer?"

"John has been arrested. He held up Lord Cochrane's coach on the Great North Road near Hatfield."

CHAPTER THREE

GRANVILLE STRODE ACROSS the room, his annoyance palpable. "Is there any tea left?"

Juliana's eyes widened, reflecting her astonishment. His brother was arrested and all he could think of was his tea! And Lady Alynwick was just as bad, sitting there pouring out a cup for him as though nothing untoward had happened. They were all mad!

"Do sit down, Spencer, and tell us what happened before Juliana swoons. Was it a wager?"

"No. John says it was ... *poetic justice*," Granville told them, accepting the cup his aunt proffered. "He and that imbecilic George Somerset took it upon themselves to teach Lord Cochrane a lesson."

"Oh, dear. Of all people to provoke. Such a nasty little man, with that vile tongue of his. Whatever possessed Johnny?"

The earl sighed. "He and Somerset were in Boodle's on Friday, when Francis Pindar came in. He'd just returned to Town and had been set upon by a masked highwayman. Pindar was in a state, still terrified, and it came to light that he hadn't put up a struggle. Just handed over his purse. Well, you know how vicious Cochrane can be. He started in on Pindar. I believe he suggested a yellow coat would become him."

"Gad! I am surprised Francis didn't call him out."

"He was too mortified. Naturally, John stepped into the fray, goading Cochrane. Said he could just see Percy throwing his quizzing glass at a highwayman or pricking him with his pretty walking stick. Cochrane reportedly declared *he* would die before surrendering his purse to a thief. He told everyone he keeps a loaded pistol in his carriage and would have no mercy on anyone who dared waylay him." The earl paused, sipping his tea. "Need I go on?"

"No. Johnny would deem it a challenge—impossible to think otherwise." She turned to Juliana. "The dear boy cannot bear to see anyone weaker or smaller taken advantage of. *Noblesse oblige* and all that."

"But what happened?" Juliana cried, ignoring Georgia's unorthodox views. "Did Lord Cochrane fire on him? Is he all right?"

"Of course he is, child," Georgia said, patting her hand. "Else Spencer would not be sitting here so calmly. How sweet of you to be concerned."

"I apologize, Miss Chevron, if I unduly alarmed you. Shall I finish the tale?" At her nod, the earl continued, "My brother and Somerset decided between them to hold up Cochrane and test his mettle. They apparently felt it would be unsporting for two men to set upon his carriage, and tossed a coin for the honour. Johnny won."

"Naturally," Georgia agreed, her eyes sparkling with pride.

"They knew Cochrane was heading North and waited for him just outside Hatfield. When his coach appeared, Johnny spurred his horse and charged out, blocking the road and firing one of his pistols in the air. There was no trouble ordering the driver to rein in. Cochrane's servants are not precisely devoted to him, and he's too clutch-fisted to hire postillions, so it was just the driver and groom."

"It would not have mattered to Johnny if there had been a dozen men," Georgia anxiously assured Juliana.

The earl directed a look of pure exasperation at his aunt. "Must you sound so approving? If you would refrain from encouraging him in these starts—"

"Don't turn fusty now, Spencer darling," Georgia cajoled, tapping him on the knee with her fan. "You may scold all you wish later, but finish the tale first. I vow it is prodigiously exciting."

"As you will." He sighed. "Johnny rode round to the side and demanded the owner step out. There was no one to be seen in the window, and no movement inside. He ordered the groom down to open the door and they saw Cochrane cowering on the floor. Johnny demanded he throw out his pistol, and then his purse. Cochrane tossed them out at once and, still on his knees, was begging for mercy. Johnny left the pistol, which proved to be unloaded, and the purse lying in the road. Whipping off his mask, he laughed and presented his compliments to Cochrane."

"Impudent, foolish boy. Why didn't he just take the purse and be off?" Georgia demanded.

"You know Johnny better than that. He laughed at Cochrane, advising him not to be mocking Pindar when his own courage was so faint as to be nonexistent, and then turned and rode off."

"Oh, that was well done of him! I would have loved to have seen it. Can you not just picture it, my dear?"

Juliana smiled. "Yes, certainly, and how utterly delightful to think you would betroth me to such a gentleman." She glanced at the earl, surprised to see a warm look of approval in his eyes. "I begin to see what you are up against, my lord. But tell me, how did Lord John come to be arrested?"

"My brother says it was cursed ill luck." He rode back to where Somerset waited for him. The pair of them dallied there, laughing over Cochrane, and drinking the champagne Somerset brought for the occasion. While they were enjoying themselves, Cochrane gathered his purse and pistol and fled. He chanced on a Robin Redbreast less than a mile later and demanded the fellow ride back and arrest John."

"Forgive my ignorance, my lord, but what is a Robin Redbreast?"

"Of course you would not know, not being accustomed, as we are, to dealing with the law. It's what the Bow Street horse patrol is called." At Juliana's look of puzzlement, he added, "They wear scarlet waistcoats."

"I see, and this man rode back and found Lord John and his friend blithely drinking champagne. Surely he must have realized your brother was not a common highwayman?"

"So one would think. But there was Cochrane jumping up and down, hysterically demanding an arrest, and John and Somerset too much in spirits to behave sensibly. The upshot was they were all dragged back to London. Of course as soon as Cochrane admitted that his purse was returned, Johnny was released. My brother thought it prudent to advise me of what had occurred and was waiting at the house when I returned this morning."

"Very thoughtful of Johnny," his aunt approved. "I hope you weren't hard on him, Spencer. I daresay it was not a proper thing to do, but I have never liked

Percy Cochrane and it's high time someone put the dreadful man in his place."

"John is on his way to Southwell. Thomas writes the stable there is in need of repairs and he can tend to that. He takes Somerset with him, and should be gone from London at least a month." The earl set his cup down and leaned forward to address Juliana. "Well, Miss Chevron, has this business given you second thoughts? I own I would not blame you were you to take your leave as soon as may be."

"Spencer! What you are saying? You cannot think Juliana would take Johnny into dislike merely for teaching that odious Cochrane a lesson." She plied her fan vigourously, assuring Juliana, "It was not just a boyish prank—it was a . . . an act of chivalry."

Juliana, her eyes full of merriment, answered gravely. "Anyone could see that, ma'am." She nodded to Granville. "I will accept the terms of our agreement, my lord, but I beg you not to mention this act of chivalry to Anna. I fear she would not see it in precisely that light."

"And would you allow the opinion of your old nurse to weigh with you?" he asked, a hint of curiosity in his blue eyes.

"Anna is the closest thing I have to family, sir, and certainly I trust her judgement."

"Then I promise to mind my tongue. Now then, if you are agreeable, Miss Chevron, I think we should plan to remove to Chelmsford at once. Will the day after tomorrow suit you?"

"Darling, you cannot be serious. I cannot pack in such a time, and I have engagements—" Georgia broke off at the look in his eyes. "Oh, very well. Juliana, my dear, I beg you will not think ill of us for travelling in such a hurlyburly fashion."

Granville answered for her. "If Miss Chevron can accept a highwayman for her intended without blinking an eye, I am certain she can see the need for haste."

"Really, Spencer, I know you are only funning, but I wonder at your sense of humour. A highwayman, when you know Johnny only—yes, Grim, what is it?" she asked as the butler tapped on the door and begged pardon for intruding.

"Princess Esterhazy and Lady Sefton have arrived, my lady. They are waiting in the Blue Room."

"Thank you, I shall be there in just a moment." She rose gracefully, giving both her hands to Juliana. "I am sorry, my dear, but I must see these ladies. It would not do to offend them, for we shall have need of them when we return to Town. They are both patronesses of Almack's, you know. Now, do not allow Spencer to overset you with his nonsense."

"I shall try not to," Juliana promised, unable to imagine the earl spouting any sort of nonsense.

JULIANA RETURNED HOME in a highly bemused state, which clearly puzzled the earl. He had quite expected her to refuse the position when she learned of John's latest hare-brained scheme, but she'd seemed only amused. Nor had she looked the least daunted when he had moved up their departure date.

Anna could have enlightened him. One look at the glow in Juliana's eyes was sufficient for her to see how the wind was blowing. It was a far cry from the pinched, weary look Juliana had worn when she turned up on their doorstep a month ago, poor lass. Life had not been kind to her darling girl.

Anna listened with patience while Juliana described her encounter with Lady Alynwick, and then detailed the delights in store for her at the earl's country seat. A dresser would cut and style her hair in the latest fashion. Two, not one, but two modistes had been engaged to fit her with a new wardrobe. A dancing master would teach her the steps to the Scottish reel dances, and the earl would teach her to drive a team.

"And then," she sighed, her green eyes dreamy, "if the earl judges me ready, we return to London and Lady Alynwick will introduce me to the ton. She is already working on procuring vouchers for me to Almack's. Oh, Anna, I wish you had met her. She is the most delightful creature, and if Lord John is anything like her, I shall adore him."

Anna said nothing. However much she might deplore the earl's plan, she could not bear to dampen Juliana's spirits. At last, she would be given the sort of Season her grandfather should have provided her years ago. The old curmudgeon had been too wrapped up in his own self to care about Juliana.

Anna recalled all too clearly the general's only effort to see to his granddaughter's future. A few months before his death, he'd proposed Juliana wed Sir Waldo Lewes. That Sir Waldo was portly and old enough to be her grandfather had not weighed with the general. Nor had it occurred to him that a young miss would find Sir Waldo's pockmarked face hideous. All he could see was that the man had a tidy estate which marched with his own lands. When his granddaughter refused the match, he'd told her she was a fool, just like her mama, and washed his hands of her.

When the general died, leaving Juliana destitute, Sir Waldo had repeated his offer. Although Juliana refused him, he'd had the decency to help her obtain a post as companion to old Lady Bideford. Poor Juliana. Her letters had not said much, but it was clear to Anna that she'd been treated as little more than a menial. The position which had followed, governess to Mrs. Staples's boisterous girls, had been little better. Four girls in her charge, and not an ounce of discipline among them. Daughters of a wealthy Cit, they were outrageously spoiled and had treated Juliana shamefully, though she was better born than them all.

No, Anna thought, watching Juliana bubbling with excitement, she'd not say a word. This post, for all its oddity, was a vast improvement. Of course, if the earl had been a different sort of man, she'd not be keeping her tongue between her teeth. She'd been around the nobility enough to be recognizing a true gentleman, and that's what Lord Granville was, no matter what anyone else might say. Even a bit strait-laced, he was, with a sad look in his eyes which told of trouble. No doubt from that young brother of his. Pity it wasn't the earl needing a wife. She'd trust Juliana to him. He was the sort a body could depend on.

Anna kissed her charge good-night, reminding her she must be up early in the morning, if she wished to do some shopping before leaving for Chelmsford.

Juliana nodded, but continued to sit at the kitchen table with only Mouser and her thoughts for company. William and the boys had gone to bed long since. Dear, good William, who had taken her aside earlier. She smiled, recalling his earnest face.

"If an you find that place ain't to your likin', Miss Juliana, you just send me a letter by way of the penny post and me and the boys will be there to bring you home again before you can blink twice."

It was a comforting thought, though she doubted William's old dray would make it as far as Chelmsford and back.

Juliana rose, gave Mouser a saucer of milk and tidied the tiny kitchen before retiring to the narrow bed the boys normally shared. She could see their red heads at the far end of the front room where they sprawled on the floor. The boys would soon have their bed back, while she would be sleeping—where? Her mind drew a blank as she tried to picture the bedchambers at Crowley. Would they be furnished with solid, heavy oak as dignified as the earl? Or filled with colours and brightness like Georgia? She finally fell asleep, her mind alternating between pleased anticipation and nervous dread.

Willie's gleeful shout woke her early the next morning. She dressed rapidly and entered the kitchen to find it a hub of excitement. The earl had sent a messenger with two letters. One was for Juliana, and lay in the centre of the table. The other, which Tommy and William were peering at over Anna's shoulder, was a commission to haul several large pieces of furniture to Chelmsford.

Anna blinked rapidly. The pound notes enclosed were far in excess of the normal fee and more than enough to keep her family housed and fed for several weeks. Bless the man.

Juliana echoed her thoughts. She would have to remember to thank Lord Granville. This was a kindness she had not looked for. She smiled at Anna. "But what was Willie on about? Never tell me he was in high gig over a commission?"

William snorted. "Not that boy. He ain't got enough sense to know what butters his bread."

"It was the messenger, Miss Juliana," Tommy put in. "Him that brung the letters."

Juliana lifted her brows as she drew out a chair. Either it was too early in the morning for her mind to properly function or she had missed something.

"Lord Granville sent his letters with a young man who helps to train his hounds," Anna enlightened her. "He's out there now with Willie trying to teach that mongrel some proper manners. Lord help him for it's a fruitless task, but it was good of the earl to remember his promise."

"Self-preservation," Juliana said, laughing, helping herself to the pot of coffee and eyeing the other letter with trepidation.

"Go on, child, see what it is," Anna urged, watching her.

Juliana lifted the cream-coloured envelope with its rich embossing. It was fortunate the earl need not worry over postal charges for it laid heavy in her hand. She unfolded the crisp linen stationery and gasped aloud at the stack of pound notes which fell out on the table.

"Blimey! There must be a hundred pounds there," Tommy said, reaching out to touch a note.

"Get your grubby hands away," Anna said, slapping at his fingers. "What does the letter say, Juliana?"

"He writes that as I may wish to purchase a few trifles before we leave, he has enclosed my salary. Anna, it *is* a hundred pounds!"

"Why's she crying, Pa? I wouldn't be sheddin' no tears if an someone was to send me a hundred pounds!" Tommy said, staring at the tears running unchecked down Juliana's cheeks.

JULIANA CHERISHED the memory of that last day with Anna and her family. She would keep it with her, like a talisman, to lift her spirits whenever she was feeling low. Her excitement over this new position was tempered by her knowledge of the realities of earning her salary. Being employed by the earl, however, was unlike anything she had yet experienced. Her first surprise was the huge fourgon which arrived early Wednesday morning to collect her trunks. It was fortunate she had only the one, for betwixt the earl and his aunt, there was little room left. The liveried footman who accompanied the huge coach informed her the earl and Lady Alynwick would come for her within an hour or two.

Juliana wondered what subterfuge Granville had used to entice Lady Alynwick on the road at such an early hour. She would warrant Georgia was not accustomed to being out and abroad at eleven in the morning. Indeed, when they arrived, the lady's sleepy-eyed greeting gave only a hint of her usual vivacious manner.

One glance round the muddy yard persuaded Lady Alynwick to remain in the carriage, and Juliana, conscious of keeping her waiting, hurriedly said her goodbyes. She kept the tears which threatened at bay, reminding herself she would not be very far off, and William could always fetch her home again in the shining new dray he was planning to buy. She hugged both the boys, their faces turning as red as their hair, and scratched Cyclops behind the ears. The large pup wiggled and whined, but sat docilely beside his young master—an accomplishment which had Willie grinning from ear to ear at the earl, who winked at him behind Juliana's back.

Lord Granville, in spite of the damp and overcast weather, was mounted on a high-bred blood horse which drew lavish cries of admiration from the boys. The earl controlled him with a seemingly effortless grace which Juliana recognized as the mark of a superb horseman. The animal snorted his impatience, and she hurried to take her seat opposite Georgia in the luxurious travelling chaise.

Leaning out the window with a tremulous smile, she waved goodbye to Anna and the boys until the yard was out of sight. Catching a glimpse of the earl watching her, she withdrew her head and settled back against the squabs.

Georgia half opened her eyes, remarking lazily, "Dear child, to look at you, one would think you are on the way to the hanging cross. I promise you Crowley is delightful and you will enjoy it amazingly. Even at this ungodly hour."

Juliana managed a small laugh. "I thought ladies of the nobility never stirred before noon."

"They do not. Particularly if they attended three balls, two routs and a late supper the evening before and did not return home till near three."

"Three in the morning! Gracious, I wonder that you were ready this morning. I would probably still be sleeping soundly."

"So would I had not my officious nephew bribed my servants," Georgia confessed. "Claudia woke me and gave me a cup of chocolate before ever I knew the time, and they all conspired to have me dressed and waiting when Spencer arrived."

"Did he truly bribe your servants?"

"No, although I've no doubt he would have done so if necessary, but they are all devoted to him. He has a way with servants and children," Georgia murmured, closing her eyes again.

Juliana glanced out of the window at the straight back of Lord Granville. He had certainly won over Anna, and both the boys thought him top-of-the-trees. William had thanked him profusely for the commission, but the earl had declaimed, maintaining the debt was on his side. An honest carter was difficult to find, he'd said... and abruptly changed the subject when he'd seen Juliana watching him. What had motivated his kindness, she wondered, and then chided herself. She was letting her experiences of the past two years turn her cynical. There did not *have* to be a reason for kindness.

Georgia snored quietly and Juliana soon followed her example, leaning her head against the squabs and allowing her mind to drift. The overcast day and the warmth and comfort of the carriage lulled her. She fell fast asleep and did not wake up until the carriage, abruptly stopping, jolted her.

Glancing out the window at the large double gates, Juliana did not need Georgia to tell her that they had arrived at Crowley. Rain had begun to fall in earnest, and there was not much to be seen. An unhappy omen, she thought. The earl, oblivious to the downpour, had reined in and she saw him speaking with the elderly gatekeeper. Juliana lost sight of him as the carriage swept up a wide avenue, but he was there to hand them down when the steps were lowered.

"Welcome to Crowley, Miss Chevron. I hope you will feel at home here," he said with a sweeping bow and no little measure of pride.

"She will be much more at home in out of the rain, Spencer. Don't keep us standing here," Georgia or-

dered, a delicate shiver lending credence to her words
as she hurried inside.

Juliana, with time for no more than a glimpse of the
imposing brick structure, followed her. The entrance
hall was vast with half a dozen massive Ionic columns
supporting an upper balcony. It was too dark for her
taste and did not permit one to see the details of the
domed, painted ceiling, or the oil paintings which
adorned the whole of one wall. A long line of windows ran the length of the east wall, but as these were
heavily draped in deep red velvet, they only added to
the darkness.

Lord Granville's staff was lined up to greet him, an
impressive array which stretched the length of the hall
and ranged from butler, valet, chef and housekeeper to
the maids and footmen clad in the earl's blue-and-silver
livery.

Granville spoke to each of them, and Juliana could
readily see why he was so much admired. Not only did
he recall their names, but also frequently paused to
enquire after a family member. Lady Alynwick, too,
was greeted warmly, the staff pleased to welcome her.
Only with Juliana did they show their normal reserve,
and she felt their eyes assessing her as she passed down
the line beside Georgia.

Granville was treating her as though she was a valued guest, and had introduced her as a protégée of his
aunt's. Servants, however, had keen eyes and would
know to a shilling how much her out-of-fashion walking dress and pelisse had cost. She felt like an impos-
tor and wished nothing more than to flee the room.

Piedmore, the elderly butler, said everything that was
proper but she could not be at ease with him. Mrs.
Jamison, the housekeeper, was more to her taste, and

reminded her a little of Anna. It was she who assigned Dorcas, a tall, lanky country girl, to attend Juliana, and suggested that perhaps she would like to freshen up before being shown to the drawing-room.

Juliana accepted her offer gratefully, and followed Dorcas up the winding staircase, through a long picture gallery, and down a draughty passage to her room. Whatever the servants might think of her, she had been given one of the best guest rooms overlooking the park. Dorcas pointed out the view proudly, drawing the cumbersome curtains away from the window.

It was a splendid vista, and Juliana admired it while she put off her hat and gloves. The chamber was of a rich, elegant design, but she found the dark furnishings oppressive. Although it was far grander than what she had become accustomed to, it seemed cold and unwelcoming. She did admire the dark oak bookcases which filled the walls on either side of the fireplace and went at once to examine the books contained there.

Dante's *Divine Comedy;* Chaucer's *The Book of the Duchess; Don Quixote* by Cervantes; several plays by Shakespeare including *The Comedy of Errors, The Taming of the Shrew* and *The Two Gentlemen of Verona;* and on the more serious side, several volumes by the evangelist Hannah More. Juliana scanned the titles and lifted down several of the books. None appeared to have been read, their pages still uncut and their spines never cracked. She replaced the books, remarking to Dorcas that it was a very fine collection.

"Yes, miss, and the same in all the front bedchambers. It was Lady Granville what come up with the notion. She had the cases 'specially built and ordered all them books."

"How delightful. I do appreciate good books. I shall have to visit the other rooms and see what else is available."

"Oh, no need, miss. They're the same in all the rooms."

"You do not mean *exactly* the same books?" Juliana said, laughing at such an absurdity.

"Yes, miss. The countess didn't want any of her guests getting lost and tumbling down the stairs like Mr. Plymstock did. He was trying to find the library, lookin' for something to read before he retired. Lord Hastings, him that was up to Oxford, told her what books were best and she jest ordered six of each of 'em."

"I see," Juliana murmured, appalled by such waste. She, who dearly cherished books, could not conceive of anyone buying several copies of the same volume merely for the sake of convenience.

"It was her what decorated the house, too, miss," Dorcas confided, straightening a pillow on the low settee. "Course I weren't here then, but Mrs. J. told me his lordship ain't never changed a thing since the poor Lady Countess died."

A pity, Juliana thought. Everything possible had been provided for a guest's comfort, but the rooms were of such a rigid formality that comfort was precluded. She did not care for the "Lady Countess's" taste. Well, there was one thing which would be changed. She immediately crossed the room and pulled an oval-backed chair closer to the fireplace.

"Bring the other one over here," she said, motioning to the astonished maid. "They do not do the least bit of good in that dark corner. Since Lady Granville was kind enough to provide me with books, I do not suppose she'd object to my being comfortable while I read them."

Dorcas giggled but obligingly moved the chair and then helped to shift the settee. The result was a cozy sitting area before the fire, and the room looked immensely more cheerful.

"It does look nice this way, miss—more homey-like," the girl owned, standing back to admire their efforts.

"Yes, I believe I much prefer it." Juliana nodded.

"If you are ready now, miss, I'll show you the way to the drawing-room. His lordship will be thinkin' we lost our way."

"Oh, heavens yes. I'd quite forgotten he would be waiting." She quickly tidied her hair and then with one last, swift touch, disarranged the orderly pillows on the sofa.

Feeling better for that small touch of rebellion, Juliana followed the giggling Dorcas through the maze of galleries. The halls seemed endless but the maid stood back at last, pointing to a door. The earl and Lady Alynwick, she said, would be in the small drawing-room.

Juliana stepped in, the words of greeting dying on her lips. The *small* room was of astonishing proportions, but what stunned her was the life-size portrait which dominated the room. Hung on the wall facing the door, the picture immediately drew the eye to the beautiful, if soberly clad, young woman. She looked down on the occupants of the room with a regal disdain. *Dear Cynthia.*

CHAPTER FOUR

THE EARL, ACCUSTOMED TO the effect Cynthia's portrait had on guests, crossed the room to Juliana's side. With a hand beneath her elbow, he urged her forward. "Come in, Miss Chevron. Dinner will be served shortly, but we have time for a glass of sherry, or ratafia, if you prefer."

"Sherry is fine, my lord," she said, sitting down next to his aunt, her eyes still drawn to the painting. The vivid colours and rich detail were startling. Cynthia was in the room with them.

"You look stunned, my dear. I keep telling Spencer he should take that painting down. It makes everyone *so* uncomfortable."

"It's your imagination," Granville said, handing Juliana a glass. "My aunt fancies Cynthia's eyes follow her everywhere in the room." He took a few steps to the side, glancing up at the portrait, head tilted in consideration. "It is somewhat dramatic, but that is the skill of Sir Thomas. Cynthia saw the painting he did of Lady Jersey and greatly admired it. I commissioned him to paint her as a wedding present."

"It is certainly an arresting portrait," Juliana murmured, thinking Georgia was in the right of it. She could feel Cynthia's disapproval.

"Thank you." Spencer nodded, accepting her words as a compliment. He gestured to the portrait. "She had the room redecorated once the painting was hung, everything in the finest English tradition. Cynthia believed the nobility should set an example by forsaking the more outrageous Oriental and French influences.''

"Dear Cynthia never had the opportunity to travel abroad," Georgia confided. "I fear you will find her tastes rather limited."

"Not at all like yours, you mean," Spencer said, actually smiling at his aunt.

"To each his own," she said with a shrug. "What about you, Juliana? What do you think of the house?"

"It's most unusual," she answered truthfully enough, while struggling to think of something worth complimenting. "The bookcases in my room are exquisite. I do not believe I have ever seen a finer collection of books provided for guests. I am certainly looking forward to reading them."

Juliana saw the quick turn of Granville's head and knew she'd surprised him.

"You enjoy reading, Miss Chevron?"

"Indeed, yes. Are you familiar with the work of Sir Richard Steele, my lord? He wrote, 'Reading is to the mind what exercise is to the body,' and just now my mind sorely needs exercising. My last employer kept few books in the house besides the latest Gothics or Lord Byron's poems."

Georgia laughed, taking Juliana's hand in her own. "Darling; you must never own to reading anything of a serious nature. It makes the gentlemen so nervous, doesn't it, Spencer?"

"Not *all* gentlemen. You are at liberty to read what you choose, Miss Chevron, and of course my library is at your disposal while you are here. Only... I believe you would be wise to refrain from mentioning your literary preferences to Johnny when you meet him."

"Don't be so discreet, Spencer. Literary preferences indeed, when you know he never opens a book of his own volition. No, don't frown at me. Juliana must learn Johnny's faults as well as his more admirable qualities. Not that it is a fault precisely. I am sure I know a dozen or more gentlemen who don't choose to spend their hours reading. I myself seldom open a book."

Juliana could almost feel sorry for the earl. He looked embarrassed by his aunt's frankness and more than a little relieved when the dinner gong sounded.

Excluding her stay with Anna, Juliana had never dined *en famille*. Her grandfather was of the school which believed children should be relegated to the nursery until they learned civilized behaviour. By the time he deemed Juliana old enough to have learned proper manners, her mother had died and he took most of his meals in his own room. She continued to eat with Anna in the nursery wing, save the rare occasions when company visited Carisbrook and she was required to act as her grandfather's hostess. Those, of course, were formal occasions.

The earl told her, guiding her down the hall, that it was his custom to use the smaller dining-room when only family were present. It might have been slightly smaller than the state dining-room, but the table, even with all the leaves removed, was still large enough to sit above a dozen people. Like the rest of the house, the room was dominated by large, heavy furniture and the curtains were pulled against the afternoon sun. The room would have been quite dark, even at the early hour of six, had not it been brilliantly lit with candles.

Georgia saw her astonishment and spoke across the table as they were seated. "Cynthia knew a thing or two. Candlelight is far more flattering to a woman than harsh sunlight."

Granville stood at the head of the table, dark brows drawn together in a frown. "While it may afford you a great deal of amusement to mock Cynthia, though I am at a loss to know what she ever did to earn your censure, I will remind you that Crowley was her home. I will not tolerate having her memory maligned in this house."

"Oh, do sit down, Spencer, and try not to behave so foolishly. Gracious, how you take on so. I was merely *complimenting* dear Cynthia."

Juliana choked down her laughter at Georgia's innocent pose, but the earl did not look amused.

"Implying that Cynthia's complexion was such that she required flattering light is hardly my notion of a compliment," he said dryly, taking his seat.

"No, of course not, darling. I was only saying she was *clever* enough to realize the need, and you must know many women never understand that. They think they don't age—"

"She was only nineteen," he pointed out, biting his lip to keep from smiling.

"Of course, Spencer. I wasn't speaking of Cynthia but only of women generally. Really, you mustn't take things so to heart. What will Juliana think of us, quarrelling over something so silly?"

Juliana wisely kept her eyes down and pretended an inordinate interest in the turtle soup before her, but she could not quite keep her lips from curving into a smile, and Granville noted her amusement.

The earl waited until the footman removed his soup, replacing it with a plate of salmon, before he spoke. "It's as well I must return to Town in the morning. I should not wish my presence to hamper your entertainment. The pair of you have much in common."

Georgia instantly looked contrite, peeping up at him from beneath her lashes. "I *am* sorry, Spencer. Truly, I did not mean to offend you. You used to share my sense of humour before—"

"Before I married Cynthia?" he finished for her in a slow, measured tone. "I also used to ride neck-or-nothing, wager excessively, drink till dawn and take pleasure in baiting the watch, but I have outgrown those pastimes. I believe the process is called maturing."

"There is such a thing as growing overly mature," Georgia countered blithely. "What happens to fruits, and yes, even eggs when they age too much?"

"Ah, now I am to be compared to a rotten egg? Gad, but there are times I wished I lived in the age where women knew their place and men were masters of their fate." He looked to Juliana for sympathy and saw her dimple, her lips curving into a mischievous smile. "Yes, Miss Chevron? You might as well say whatever thought has amused you. It cannot be worse than what my aunt would say of me."

"It was only the rest of that quotation, my lord."

He looked startled, but comb his memory as he might, could not think of the reference. "Enlighten us, my dear."

"It was from *Julius Caesar*. 'Men at some times are masters of their fates: The fault, dear Brutus, is not in our stars, but—"

"In ourselves," he finished. "Yes, I rather asked for that."

Georgia laughed. "Oh, it is going to be delightful having you in the family, dearest. I can never score a hit when Spencer turns literary on me."

"My only defence against your illogical logic," Granville said, taking a sip of wine. He looked up to find Juliana regarding him, an odd light in her green eyes. "What now, Miss Chevron?"

"Nothing, my lord," she demurred, looking down at her plate.

"Come now, as my aunt says, you are to be part of the family. You must not be reticent. What was it you wished to know?"

"I was just trying to picture you riding neck-or-nothing and baiting the watch," she confessed, and when he did not immediately look offended, dared further. "Did you really, my lord?"

A slow smile transformed his face, and the pale blue eyes took on a liveliness which made him look years younger. "I did a number of vastly foolish things which I hope have long been forgotten. I fear my colleagues in the House of Lords would not listen with such flattering attention to my speeches were they to recall some of my misdeeds. 'But I content myself with wishing that I may be one of those whose follies cease with their youth, and not of that number who are ignorant in spite of their experience.'"

"I hope you are not so impertinent as to intend that remark for my benefit," Georgia said, motioning to the footman to refill her glass and giving her nephew a dark look.

"I rather think he's getting his own back," Juliana said, laughing. "I confess my ignorance. Who wrote those lines, sir?"

"It was a bit unfair," he admitted. "William Pitt spoke those words in the House of Commons when Walpole charged him with 'the atrocious crime of being a young man.' A friend of my grandfather's was present that day and Pitt made quite an impression on him. My grandfather told me the story once and for some odd reason, the words stayed in my mind."

"Not only unfair, but hardly appropriate, my lord," Juliana said, her eyes seeming to twinkle in the candlelight.

"How is that, Miss Chevron? We were speaking of the follies of my youth."

"If memory serves me, William Pitt was in his early thirties when he debated Walpole—somewhere near your own age, my lord? And charged with being a *young* man?"

"Touché, my dear," he said, his blue eyes regarding her with warm approval. "You have a quick mind."

Juliana was near to blushing, absurdly pleased by the earl's casual compliment. Georgia, however, was not and took her young protégée to task.

"My dear, do not encourage him to draw you into such conversations. Spencer may think quoting greybeards long since in their graves, and better left there in my opinion, to be witty, but I assure you, most of the ton does not. Were it to get about that you were a bluestocking, we would be undone."

Juliana met the earl's eyes in a moment of shared amusement, but quickly assured Georgia that she would mind her tongue, and the remainder of the meal passed in a lighthearted manner. The schedule for the following day was discussed, beginning what Georgia referred to as Juliana's training to become the perfect lady.

THE EARL LEFT FOR LONDON early the next morning, and Juliana barely had time to give his absence a thought, though his name was mentioned frequently. Georgia was a gruelling taskmaster and kept her far too occupied to think of anything but the role she was playing.

Mr. Lafoy himself, London's renowned hairdresser to the haut ton, arrived at Crowley to cut and style Juliana's hair. Fortunately, he was of the belief that a lady's best hairstyle was what became her the most. He cut only the top and sides, and trimmed her long hair so it fell in becoming waves. By day, she wore it down with silk ribbons, matching the colour of her gown, entwined in her curls. For evening, the lustrous waves were brushed back away from her brow and pulled into a topknot of delicate curls.

The two modistes engaged by the earl were bitter rivals, and each was committed to outdoing the other in fashioning Miss Chevron's wardrobe. Mornings were spent in long hours of fittings, and Juliana would stand still for hours at a time while the ladies poked and prodded at her slender form until she thought she would scream. The torture proved worth it when three days later, Madame Letitia produced the first of the dinner dresses. Lady Alynwick was summoned and Juliana nervously modelled it.

The dress, in the style of the day, had an extremely low, square-cut neckline, a high waistline and sleek, flowing lines. The underdress was a satin slip of deep green, covered by a soft emerald green netting. Juliana delighted in the luxurious feel of the fabrics and excellent fit, but the revealing décolletage left her uneasy, and she appealed to Georgia, who chided her for her foolishness.

"It is perfect, child. Not a gentleman in London will be able to resist you in that gown."

"But the neckline—" Juliana protested, bringing a hand up to her throat.

"It's the style, darling. Be thankful you have the figure to wear it and do so proudly. Shoulders back, Juliana. That's better. You must strive not to look embarrassed or you shall spoil the effect."

Madame Camillia, not pleased to have her rival complete the first dress, harried her minions and completed Juliana's morning dress only hours later. It was a pretty shade of dark orange. Capucine, *madame* called it, and Georgia declared it divine against Juliana's dark hair.

Several more outfits were completed in the following days. Walking dresses, carriage dresses, evening gowns, a theatre dress, an opera gown, and more day dresses. Juliana protested she could never wear so many clothes, but both the modistes and Georgia ignored her. The earl had given his aunt carte blanche, and she was enjoying herself enormously, unlike Juliana, who escaped to the stables whenever she could.

Madame Letitia had provided her with a beautifully tailored dark blue riding habit. It was Juliana's favourite of all her new clothes, and she looked forward to the hour in the afternoon when she was usually free to ride. Granville had left instructions that she was to be suitably mounted, and Ian, his head groom, had given her a choice of three perfectly mannered mares.

She had tried each of their paces and settled on Lady-slipper, a delicate well-bred chestnut.

Ian, a short and stocky dour Scot, gave her his be-grudging approval. Ladyslipper was the best of the mares, and Juliana rode her with a good seat and light hands. He was heard to remark to the undergroom that Miss Chevron knew one end of the horse from the other, which was more than he could say for some ladies—an oblique reference to Cynthia, who had squealed in terror when a mare had playfully nudged her shoulder.

The afternoon was warm and sunny, and Juliana felt her spirits lifting as she neared the stables. Ian had her mare waiting, and she greeted him warmly, stooping to pet a tan spaniel sitting quietly at his heels.

"I was beginning to think there were no dogs at Crowley," she said to Ian as she caressed the silky ears. The animal looked up at her with large, sad eyes and gratefully nuzzled her hand.

Ian said nothing, waiting patiently to give her a leg up on the mare, and after a moment, Juliana allowed him to help her mount. She leaned forward, patting Ladyslipper's neck, and then looked round. She was pleased to see it was Alwyn, Ian's oldest boy, who would ride with her today. Once away from his fa-ther's disapproving eyes, he was like a bottle suddenly uncorked and words spewed forth endlessly.

Juliana, enjoying the ride and admiring the beauti-ful park which surrounded Crowley, listened with half an ear as he prattled on about the new Thoroughbred his lordship intended to race at Newmarket. It was one Lord Johnny had brought back with him from Ire-land, and she knew she should pay more attention, but racing did not really interest her. Not when the sky was so blue, and the sun warm on her face.

"Did you see the new litter of pups, miss? They belong to Ginger, the spaniel you was petting in the yard. Four little ones, she's got. Do you like dogs, miss?"

"Yes, of course," she answered lazily.

"Lady Granville didn't. That's how come there ain't any up at the house. She didn't like dogs or horses, not even cats. Pa says his lordship always had a passel of spaniels at his boots till he married her. Pa says the earl's got a way with dogs and horses, too. Pa says it's a rare thing in a gentleman, but his lordship's got the gift."

"The gift?" she asked.

He nodded. "You know, someone who can understand animals and talks to them and make 'em do what he wants."

She thought of Cyclops and smiled. "Not always, I'm afraid."

"Oh, yes, miss. He always did. Lord Johnny's got it, too, but not so much and more with jest the horses."

She didn't answer him as they neared the lane, but when she entered the yard and saw the spaniel sitting by the stable doors, she remembered the pups. Ian was there to help her dismount, and on impulse, she asked if she could see the new litter.

He said nothing for a moment and then nodded. "Aye, Alwyn'll show 'em to you, miss."

The pups were in the tack room and Alwyn led the way. Ginger followed them in and sat proudly by the door, while Juliana knelt in the straw, laughing at the antics of the puppies. Four squirming, wiggling balls of fur. They tried to climb in her lap and up her arms to lick her face.

"They're beautiful," she said, scooping up the smallest of the litter. A soft, tan butterball with dark eyes and a pink tongue. She fondled the long ears, remembering another spaniel that had been her constant companion at Carisbrook.

Alwyn stood in the doorway watching her. She looked like an angel kneeling there and he wished there was something wonderful he could do for her, and impulsively blurted out, "You could have one if you liked."

Juliana looked up at him, a smile lighting her eyes. "Thank you, but what would I do with him?"

"Even if you couldn't keep 'im, you could take 'im up to the house, miss. His lordship wouldn't mind, and you could pretend he was yours while you was here."

She bent her head and the spaniel tried to climb up her shoulder. She caught him and held him securely against her. She could feel the warmth of his quivering body through her jacket. Such a tiny thing.

She stood up. "Perhaps I'll just take this one up and show it to Lady Alynwick, if that would be all right?"

"Oh, yes, miss," he said. It would be all right with him if Miss Chevron wanted the moon brought down.

Georgia, cutting roses in the south garden, saw Juliana crossing the lawn and called to her. "There you are, darling. I was just going to send for you. Madame Letitia has your new gown finished and wants to see it on you one last time. Oh, what have you got there?"

Juliana lifted one of the floppy ears and turned so Georgia could see the tiny spaniel half asleep in her arms. "There's a litter of pups in the stables. Did you know? I could not resist bringing this one up for you to see. Isn't he beautiful, Georgia?"

"If you say so, my love. Personally, I prefer cats, though it does have rather an appealing face. What are you going to do with it?"

"Take it back to the stable, I suppose," Juliana said, bending her head to kiss the black button nose, missing the sudden calculating look in Georgia's eyes.

"You haven't time now, darling. Why don't we keep it in the house? Spencer won't mind, I'm certain, and puppies are so amusing."

"Are you sure Lord Granville will not object?"

"Perfectly," Georgia said, cutting an elegant deep crimson rose. "And even if he should, there are ways to handle gentlemen. Let me give you some advice, my dear. I am a few years older than you—if you dare to laugh, you wretched girl, I shall not help you."

"No, no. I am sorry," Juliana protested with an unrepentant smile. "Please go on, Georgia."

"Granville is right. You have no respect for your elders."

"But you are only a very few years older—"

Georgia tapped her on the wrist with a rose. "Wicked girl. Now, heed what I say. A man—any man—is like butter in the hands of a woman who knows what she is about. You must always remember just one thing. Flattery."

Juliana waited, but Georgia was silent, intent on her roses. "I don't understand. Flattery?"

"Yes, but of course. There is not a gentleman alive who is not susceptible to flattery. My mama told me, and now I am telling you. The odd thing is that gentlemen will believe anything of a complimentary nature, no matter how outlandish, and they can never be praised enough. You would suppose that otherwise sensible, intelligent men would have a bit of common sense. But no. Let a pretty girl tell them that they are the most handsome, the most clever, the wittiest, the bravest—whatever. They will believe it and adore her for it."

"That might work with some gentlemen, but I cannot conceive of Lord Granville succumbing to flattery."

"Foolish girl. How do you think dear Cynthia trapped him? Now hurry and change. I want to see you in that new gown, and then I think we shall have just enough time for a cup of tea before you practice the ballads. Your voice is quite lovely, Juliana, but you must concentrate more on remembering the words."

JULIANA FULLY INTENDED to keep the puppy, christened Felix, in her room. He, however, had other ideas, and set up a constant howling whenever he was left alone, which drove everyone to distraction. Soon he was following her through the maze of hallways. When Juliana practiced on the harpsichord, Felix could be found sleeping serenely beneath the instrument. When she danced with Monsieur Durand, the pup watched, his tail wagging in time to the music. And when Juliana and Georgia dined, it would be only a matter of minutes before Felix managed to slip through the doors and settle contentedly beneath her chair.

Juliana knew the pup was becoming outrageously spoiled, but it was difficult to chasten an animal whose tiny body would quiver at the first harsh word, and look up at his accuser with huge, sad eyes.

When Georgia found Felix in the drawing-room, chewing an elegant peach slipper for which she had paid an enormous sum, she scolded him severely. Felix abased himself on the floor, the golden fur on his back visibly trembling, and covered his eyes with his paws. Georgia swept him up in a lavish hug. "There, poor little darling. It's quite all right. Of course you need *something* to play with," and promptly gave him her other slipper.

Even the venerable Piedmore unbent and was heard to remark to Mrs. Jamison that it was pleasant to have a dog in the house again. He appeared not to notice when the housekeeper took to carrying bits of cheese in her pocket to give the poor little fellow a treat, or when the chef set aside several delectable bones. Felix devoured them in an ecstasy of feeding which the chef declared showed his appreciation for haute cuisine.

The dignified, stately mansion known as Crowley was undergoing a subtle change. It wasn't only the introduction of the mischievous pup into the household. There was the music, too. Each afternoon Juliana's clear, sweet voice filled the rooms with the gay, lilting ballads which were Lord John's favourites. Even the maids could be heard humming the tuneful airs as they went about their work.

The small salon where Juliana practiced was filled with fresh air and sunshine. The heavy curtains were tied back each morning and the French doors set open to catch the summer breeze. At first Mrs. Jamison had looked askance. The curtains had not been opened in years.

Georgia, wrinkling her delicate nose, had remarked the room smelled musty, which was sufficient to set Mrs. Jamison to airing the entire house. The gloomy, heavy curtains were pulled back and the windows opened in all the rooms. Juliana, tactfully asking permission of the housekeeper, visited the gardens and brought in armfuls of flowers to add their sweet scent.

She showed Mrs. Jamison a way to simmer orange flower water so the enticing aroma wafted through the halls, and the rooms took on a new aura.

All that is, except the blue drawing-room where Cynthia continued to stare down in stern disapproval. By mutual consent, Juliana and Georgia avoided that room, using instead the smaller salon with its pretty green-and-white design. The harpsichord was moved there, and in the evenings Georgia played while Juliana learned the steps of the Scottish reels and country dances, the minuet and the Ecossaise. Everything but the waltz. Monsieur Durand refused to teach what he considered a disgraceful dance.

On Friday evening, Juliana descended the stairs in her new gown, a fragile creation of the palest blue satin with an overdress of a net, which shimmered with each step she took.

Georgia insisted Juliana wear her new gowns each evening, hoping the child would become accustomed to their low necklines and revealing décolletage.

"You look positively radiant, my dear," Georgia complimented her as she reached the hall. Indeed, Juliana had blossomed under her lavish care and pampering. Her green eyes sparkled and her mouth curved into an alluring smile as she swept Georgia a graceful curtsy.

"Do you think Lord Granville will be pleased?" she asked, peeping through her lashes as Georgia had taught her.

"Spencer? Why yes, of course, child. And Johnny will think you ravishing. I vow I can barely wait for him to see you."

Nor could Juliana, but she was also eager for the earl to see her transformation. She knew her new hairstyle had added an air of sophistication to her looks. Her new dresses and gowns were masterful creations and Granville had never seen her in anything but her worn, out-of-style day dresses. It was childish, she thought as she entered the drawing-room, wanting to show off her new clothes and hair, only Granville had looked at her with such condescension that first day.

Felix gave a playful bark, hating to be ignored. Georgia nodded to him, "Yes, *mon petit chou*, you are looking very handsome, too."

Juliana laughed. "I swear he understands you, Georgia. Only look how he preens himself."

Piedmore interrupted them, his stolid expression replaced by an unusually worried one. "Your pardon, Lady Alynwick, but his lordship has just returned. Do you wish me to order dinner set back?"

"Wonderful. Yes, please do, Piedmore, half an hour, and tell his lordship we are in here." She turned to Juliana, smiling encouragement. "Relax, darling, you look marvellous. But perhaps we should put Felix—"

There was no time to remove the spaniel. Piedmore opened the door again, stepping back to admit the earl. He paused inside the door, glancing round the room. He had driven down from London and still wore a dark blue riding coat, and buff pantaloons which disappeared below the knee inside black top boots. He pulled off his leather gloves, glancing from Juliana to his aunt, and back to Juliana.

"Spencer, what a delightful surprise. I had not looked for you until tomorrow," Georgia said in a rush, crossing the room to greet him.

Juliana watched him dutifully kiss his aunt's proffered cheek, but there was no warmth in his eyes. The glance he sent in her own direction could hardly be construed as admiring, and she knew with a sinking feeling that he was angry.

He greeted her with a curt nod before addressing Georgia. "I am surprised to find you in here. Was there a problem with the blue drawing room?"

"No, of course not. Only this room is more comfortable. I used to sit here in the afternoons with your mother, do you remember? Winifred always preferred this room. And you did say I should treat the house as though it were my own."

"Quite, although I hardly expected you to turn it inside out," he murmured with a pointed look at the open doors.

"It was *stuffy*, Spencer. Houses, like people, benefit from a little fresh air now and then," Georgia said, watching him closely. He was in one of his pompous moods. Usually a little needling from her was all that was needed to bring him down off his high perch. It wasn't working now. His eyes were focused on Juliana, and the glint of anger in them turned them an icy blue.

"Is that a new gown, Miss Chevron? It will have to be altered. It is hardly appropriate for the drawing-room and entirely unsuitable for a girl your age. Only a woman who has little else to offer would reveal so much of her... charms."

Georgia gasped and a mortifying blush suffused Juliana's cheeks. She lifted her chin defiantly, anger sparking in her green eyes. "Then it is entirely appropriate, my lord, since I am selling myself to the highest bidder!"

Granville took a step towards her, but stopped as a tiny ball of fur catapulted itself at him, growling fiercely.

"What the devil?" He looked down at Felix, valiantly braced on his short legs, his low growl of warning incongruous with his small, fluffy frame.

"Felix, no!" Juliana cried, swiftly kneeling beside the pup, and unconsciously offering Granville an enticing view of her creamy breasts. It was too much.

"Must I beat off a dog every time we meet, Miss Chevron? Even in my own house? Leave him."

Juliana rose hesitantly, her eyes on Granville, but he was not looking at her.

"Sit," he ordered the pup abruptly, and Felix, recognizing the voice of authority, obediently sat, tail wagging. The earl stooped, stretching out his hand for the animal to sniff, and half smiled as the pup licked his fingers. "Good boy," he said so softly that only the animal could hear. The traitorous Felix lay down, and then rolled on his back, waving his short legs in the air.

CHAPTER FIVE

GEORGIA'S LAUGHTER broke the tension. "Clever Felix, to recognize the master of the house."

Granville glanced at her. "Does this miserable excuse for a dog belong to you?"

"I am afraid he's yours," Juliana said quietly. "The spaniel in the stables had a litter, and Georgia thought you would not object to having this one in the house."

"No, of course he will not, will you, Spencer? You used to keep several dogs in the house, so I knew you would not mind one small puppy."

The earl looked down at Felix, now sitting at his feet with a hopeful air, his head tilted as he listened. "At least he has better manners than Cyclops." He looked at Juliana, his smile a rueful apology of sorts.

"Better manners than some people," she murmured and though she smiled, it was a dutiful effort. His words still rankled and she turned away.

"Miss Chevron, I fear I spoke hastily and I offer you my apologies. My words were ill chosen. I did not mean to imply—that is, what I meant to say is—"

"Oh, Spencer, you men are all alike. You found Juliana's gown vastly disturbing. So will every gentleman in London. That is the reason ladies wear such gowns." Georgia smiled at him as she sat down, a teasing light in her eyes. "Of course, I noticed you did not object to the cut of *my* gown."

"You are a good deal older," he began. An unfortunate choice of words, which he realized the instant he uttered them. Georgia deliberately turned her shoulder to him.

"Come Juliana, sit by me, dearest, and we shall plot how to repay my nephew for his insults. One would think that a gentleman who deals with royalty and ambassadors would know more of tact and diplomacy."

Juliana joined her on the sofa, ostensibly ignoring the earl, and hiding a smile. Was it really possible the cool and aloof Granville had behaved so boorishly because the cut of her gown disturbed him? The thought gave her a heady sense of power.

The earl, uninvited, took the chair opposite. Felix trotted after him and sat faithfully at his feet. He reached down to fondle the pup's long ears and spoke softly. "At least you don't misunderstand a fellow's words, do you, boy? Just because I find those two ladies too beautiful to need the added enticement of revealing gowns, I'm sent to Coventry. I mean, just look at Miss Chevron. She will blind every gentleman in London. They'll be so busy admiring her figure they won't even notice the lustre of her hair or the curve of her mouth when she smiles," he paused, his own eyes on Juliana, and then added, "Or the way her eyes light up when she is amused."

"Did you hear something, Juliana?" Georgia asked, waving her fan languidly. "Perhaps it was only my imagination. They do say that as one gets on in years, one's hearing deteriorates."

The earl stifled a choke of laughter, and continued speaking in a soft murmur to the pup. "Did you ever see anyone to compare with my aunt? I know precisely how old she is, but I still have difficulty in believing her a day over twenty. She and Miss Chevron could pass for sisters.''

"Very pretty, Spencer," Georgia approved, turning to him. "But really, darling, you must guard your tongue. There are times when you distinctly remind me of your father.''

"What? Am I beyond redemption, then?'' The third Earl of Granville had been a stiff-rumped, high stickler and his battles with his pretty sister-in-law had been legion. It was the worst she could say of anyone.

"Not yet, love, but you must take care. There are times when you get that disapproving glint in your eye and there is a certain rigidity to your manners which puts me strongly in mind of Algernon. You may well laugh, Spencer, but I promise you it quite worries me.''

"Then I offer you my most abject apologies. And you also, Miss Chevron. Will you forgive me?''

"Certainly, my lord, and I apologize in turn. In truth, I confess I had some reservations about this gown, only Georgia assured me . . .''

He was instantly contrite. There was an innocence about her and a vulnerability which made him feel the greatest beast in nature. "It is ravishing, and I was a clod to suggest otherwise. I fear I have forgotten what a London Season entails, and you must be guided by my aunt. She is much more conversant with the latest styles.''

"There, you see, Juliana. Even Spencer finds you ravishing. I told you how it would be.''

She was not entirely convinced and, recalling his words, looked at Granville doubtfully. "Are you certain, my lord?''

"Quite. I spoke hastily, Miss Chevron, and without thinking. I am afraid Cynthia's views influenced me.

She was reared rather strictly, and she disapproved of gowns which were, er..."

"Revealing," Georgia said, taking pity on him, and adding with her usual frankness, "but then, poor Cynthia did not have any reason to wear such gowns. The poor child was less than amply endowed, if you take my meaning."

Granville almost rose to the bait, but checked. Seeing Juliana blushing deeply, he comforted himself with the thought that surely someone would one day strangle his beloved, outrageous aunt. He stood. "Wasn't that the dinner gong I heard?"

"I do not think so, Spencer. I—"

"Ah, but you do not hear as well as you used to," he teased, offering her an arm.

Juliana had dined so frequently with only female companions that she did not fully realize the difference it made when a gentleman was present. Especially a gentleman as charming as the earl, when he chose to exert himself to please. Georgia sparkled, as she always did in the presence of a male, even though that gentleman was her nephew. The talk was lighthearted banter, full of double meanings and innuendo. Granville, with his quick wit, kept Juliana on her toes. When she was able to answer him in kind, she basked in the warmth of his disarming smile, and the admiration in his blue eyes.

Juliana watched him parrying thrusts with Georgia with lazy good humour and an attentiveness which was flattering. If Lord John had only one tenth his charm, she would be a very fortunate young lady. She smiled at the thought.

The earl brought his attention back to her just as she smiled. He drew in a deep breath, certain Juliana had no idea of how enticing she looked in the soft candle-light. He was careful to keep his eyes on her face and away from the provocative dark shadow which he knew lay between her breasts. Johnny, he thought, was a very fortunate young man.

"Have you learned to mind your steps?" he asked, referring to her dancing lessons with the Frenchman.

"If you please, you may judge for yourself, my lord. Georgia will play for us later, while I practice with Monsieur Durand."

"She moves divinely, Spencer. Even Durand, who is hardly given to praise, declares she has a natural grace. You will join us, won't you? We are very gay, I promise you. I play while Juliana dances and Felix keeps time to the music with his tail. You will be most amused."

Juliana glanced down at the pup, but he was not in his usual place beside her chair. Fickle beast, she thought, and then saw Granville neatly palm a piece of beef before his hand disappeared beneath the table. The earl continued talking as though nothing untoward had happened.

He declared himself eager enough to see the dancing that he was willing to forgo his usual brandy and cigar, and within a very short time they were all gathered in the green-and-white salon. The earl stretched out comfortably in an armchair near the fireplace, watching his aunt take her seat at the harpsichord with elaborate ceremony. Felix settled happily at his feet.

A footman was dispatched to tell Monsieur Durand they were ready, and the dapper Frenchman arrived minutes later. He greeted the ladies with his usual aplomb, kissing the air above their hands in the Continental manner, before making a deferential bow to the earl, and enquiring of his health. The amenities observed, he turned to Juliana.

"The minuet first, I think, *mademoiselle,*" he murmured, taking her hand. Feeling the trembling of her fingers, he whispered, "Do not be overset, Miss Chevron. Forget the earl is watching and dance as though we were alone."

It was absurd for her to be nervous, she told herself. She had danced with Monsieur Durand for hours every evening, and she was confident she knew the steps and could follow him with ease. Hearing Georgia strike the first notes, she moved hesitantly. Feeling awkward and unusually clumsy, she knew she must concentrate on the music and not the pair of pale blue eyes watching from across the room. It was a few minutes before she relaxed enough to move gracefully through the steps, and then she forgot everything except her enjoyment in the dance. She was surprised to hear the sound of applause when the minuet ended.

"Well done, my dear," the earl called from his chair, and Felix thumped his tail enthusiastically.

Juliana curtsied, thankful for the cool breeze coming in from the garden. Her cheeks felt warm and flushed with her triumph. She was given no opportunity to rest, however. Georgia at once switched to a Scottish reel, and Juliana took up her position. There was no faltering or hesitation this time. She executed the steps with an inner joy which was a pleasure to watch.

She danced for the better part of an hour, and Monsieur Durand was moved to declare she no longer needed an instructor. He bowed formally to her, before escorting her to Georgia's side.

"Your protégée is ready to make her debut, Lady Alynwick. There is not a lady in London, barring yourself, who dances with such exquisite grace."

Georgia gave him her hand, along with a flirtatious look from beneath her long lashes. "Thank you, *monsieur*. You have done a marvellous job with Juliana."

"Ah, *madame,* I have done nothing but show her the way. She is part French, and has the natural inclination. That I cannot teach. It must be bred within, you understand?"

"Really, *monsieur?* Then it is unkind of you to say so, sir, when you know I have no French blood in my veins."

"You may be English by birth, *madame,* but you have the soul of a French coquette," he assured her, smiling. "And now I must say *adieu.* I return to London in the morning."

The earl had risen and strolled over to join the group round the harpsichord. "A flawless performance, *monsieur*. Both you and Miss Chevron are to be commended. But what of the waltz? Is that not in your repertoire?"

The Frenchman drew himself up, affronted. "I, Maurice Claude Durand, do not teach so indelicate a dance. What do the Germans know of beauty and grace? The waltz! Bah, it is a passing fancy which will never be accepted by the true aristocracy. Do not waste your time learning the ridiculous steps for it will be gone like that," he said, snapping his fingers.

Georgia politely waited until he had left the room before remarking, "A pity he is so small-minded. I'd no idea he was so set against the waltz, though I suppose I should have had an inkling when Augusta Lichfield recommended him so highly. She, you know, disapproves of it strongly and refused to allow her daughters to dance it."

"Small wonder," Granville said, taking a pinch of snuff. "Lady Lichfield is a woman of superior sense. She knows her girls are both too large to waltz. It takes a slender, graceful figure to perform the steps without appearing foolish." His eyes lingered on Juliana. "Someone like Miss Chevron."

Georgia's fingers struck the notes of a waltz, strongly marking the time. "Well, she must learn. She has never danced it and you know Johnny adores waltzing. Show her the steps, Spencer."

Juliana, feeling unaccountably nervous, blushed as the earl bowed before her, and took her right hand in his.

"Relax, Miss Chevron. It is a delightful dance, and save Monsieur Durand, there are few persons who oppose it," he said, silently apologizing to Cynthia, who had most definitely disapproved of the waltz. He stood beside her, slowly walking her through the steps.

Juliana wondered how she could ever follow him. How would she know in which direction he intended to move? She would be mortified if she trod on his boots.

Granville moved in front of her, directing her to place her left hand on his shoulder. She did so and felt his right arm move around her, his hand resting on the small of her back. She had never been held so intimately in her life, and could not meet his eyes. This was nothing like dancing with Monsieur Durand.

"Allow my hand to guide you," Granville said, his voice soft in her ear. "Listen to the rhythm of the music."

Juliana kept her eyes on her feet as she went down the room by his side, experiencing a slightly dizzy sensation as he twirled her round, and she twice missed her step. Relieved when the music stopped, she instantly moved away from him.

"Try it again, Juliana," Georgia called. "You have the basic form but you look as though you have the toothache. You are supposed to be *enjoying* yourself, darling."

Granville took her hand again, and this time his clasp was not so strange. She forced herself to concentrate on her steps and listen to the music. Gradually, the rhythm of the waltz worked its magic and she relaxed slightly in his arms.

"Look at me, Miss Chevron," Granville murmured. "Not only must you follow the steps, but you are required to converse with your partner. Delightful weather for this time of the year, is it not?"

She glanced up, expecting to see derision in his eyes, but met only a warm look of encouragement. "Exceptionally, my lord," she managed before gasping as he whirled her expertly in a small circle. His hand on her back guided her and when they completed the turn without mishap, she felt a rush of exhilaration.

"Wonderful!" Georgia applauded. "A little more practice and you shall do splendidly. Shall we try it one more time?"

"Tomorrow will do," Granville said. "Miss Chevron must surely be tired, and there are some papers I must attend to. If you ladies will excuse me?" He scarcely gave them time to reply, and was gone before Georgia could protest.

Juliana did not know whether she felt more relieved or disappointed, and smiled ruefully. "Perhaps I trod on his toes too many times."

"Nonsense, child. Had you danced perfectly, he still would have left us. Spencer is too conscientious. He always puts his work above personal enjoyment."

It was fortunate for Georgia's peace of mind that she did not look in on her nephew. Granville had settled himself at his desk in the library, but he was not working on the papers spread before him. He sat, smoking a cigar, and gazing out the window at the darkness beyond. It was some minutes before he realized Felix had followed him, and felt the spaniel's paw on his knee.

"Hello, fellow," he said, fondling the dog's floppy ears. "And what did you think of that exhibition? Yes, she dances wonderfully, but that gown is a damnable distraction, isn't it? And she hasn't the slightest notion of what it does to a man. Poor John—I think his bachelor days are numbered." But there wasn't the slightest trace of sympathy in his voice.

GRANVILLE WAS an habitually early riser, and though he had spent a restless night, he was still the first one down for breakfast. He paused at the door of the dining room, blinking against the uncustomary brightness. The curtains were drawn back, flooding the room with sunlight. The heavy silver epergne, normally standing in the centre of the table, had been moved to the sideboard. In its place was a low bowl of freshly cut flowers.

Mrs. Jamison came in with a pot of coffee as he took his seat and opened his newspaper.

"Morning, my lord. It's a lovely day, sir, so sunny and bright."

"Thank you. I had deduced as much," he said tartly, nodding at the open curtains.

"An advantage, ain't it, sir? I mean, knowing what it's like before you step outside and all. And cheerful, too. Makes a body feel good to see the sun shining and the dew on the grass sparkling."

His brows rose and he glanced at her over the top of his paper. "I had never realized you were so poetic, Mrs. Jamison."

The colour rose in her face slightly. "Truth is, sir, weren't much to be poetic about with the house always shut up so dark and all. But it was Lady Alynwick what said that about the grass."

"I see, and I suppose it was my aunt's notion to open all the curtains and fill the house with flowers, too?"

"The flowers were Miss Chevron's idea, my lord. She has a way with 'em, don't she, sir," she replied, turning the bowl on the table. "Like a flower herself, so pretty and sweet, she is."

"Is that more of my aunt's poetic musings?" he asked, rustling the paper.

"No, my lord," she said, smiling as she headed for the door. "That's what Mr. Piedmore says."

She left him to read his paper in peace, and the earl tried to concentrate on the news from London, but was finding it difficult to focus his attention. If Miss Chevron had such an unusual effect on his normally quiet household, what would she do to London? He'd finished his breakfast and the footman was refilling his coffee cup, when he became aware of a distraction in the hall. It almost sounded like someone moaning. He glanced up at the man. "What is that dreadful noise, Albert?"

"It's Maggie, my lord, tidying up." The footman was unsuccessful in hiding a grin, and had Piedmore been present, he would have been sharply reprimanded.

"Maggie? Is the girl sick?"

"No, my lord. She's singing, sort of. Since Miss Chevron's been practicing in the afternoon, Maggie's been learning the tunes and singing along like, while she does her work. Shall I send her away, sir?"

"No, I'm finished here," he said, closing the paper. A particularly high, sour note sounded from the hall. "Er, does Miss Chevron sound like that when she sings?"

"No, sir," the young man replied reverently, his eyes taking on a dreamy look. "Miss sounds like an angel."

He heard Juliana's voice and nodded decisively to the footman. Felix preceded her into the room, his tail held high and his black button nose quivering as he sniffed the air. He trotted to the earl's chair, and sat hopefully at his feet, head cocked.

Granville, without thinking, rewarded him with a piece of bacon, but his gaze was on Juliana. Mrs. Jamison's words were apt. She did look as pretty and sweet as a flower. A butterflower, he thought, eyeing the bright yellow ribbon which confined her curls, and trimmed the sleeves and bodice of her morning dress. The dress, he noted with some relief, was not so indecorously cut as the gown she'd worn the evening before.

"Good morning, my lord," she said, smiling, as he hastily rose. "I see you've joined in the conspiracy to spoil Felix."

"What? Oh, the spaniel. I'm afraid I dropped a piece of bacon. That pup eats as though he were starving."

"It's all a pose, my lord," she said, laughing. "He will resort to any lengths for an extra bite or two. Not even Cyclops behaves so shamelessly."

"Cyclops hasn't so much sense," he said, trying to ignore the doleful, pleading look in the pup's eyes. "That mongrel is progressing, however, and may one day prove to be a tolerable animal. The lad who looks after him is young yet, but he seems to have a way with dogs."

"Indeed he does, and it brings him a fair amount of trouble. Just when his father has need of him, Willie disappears to nurse some stray he found in the neighbourhood. I am afraid he has no interest in the business and William despairs of his ever learning a proper trade."

"So he said. I stopped by yesterday on my way down and had a word with him. I did not say anything to him yet—I wanted to ask your advice first—but I've a notion about the lad. Anna is fine, by the way, and sends her love to you."

If he had been looking for a reward, the glow in her eyes as she thanked him was sufficient payment. Embarrassed by her gratitude, he rose quickly, halting her words.

"There is someone I should like you to meet. His name is Alf Tyrell and he lives four or five miles south of here. If you have time, we could drive over this afternoon, and combine the visit with your first driving lesson."

"Certainly, my lord," she said, trying to curb her curiosity. "Whenever it is convenient for you. Madame Camillia leaves for London this morning, and Madame Letitia needs only one more fitting.''

''Let us say two o'clock, then.'' He nodded and left the room before she could question him further. Felix trotted halfway to the door after him, and then paused, looking back at Juliana. The pup hesitated before prancing back to her side.

''Abominable dog. You only stayed because the food is in here. You're not fooling me.''

LORD GRANVILLE'S CURRICLE was drawn round to the front of the house, and he was waiting on the steps when Juliana descended that afternoon. She still wore her yellow morning dress, but she had added a pretty straw hat with yellow plumes and a pair of short, tan leather gloves. To the casual observer, she looked delightful. Only a very close scrutiny would detect the signs of nervousness that was causing the fluttery feeling in her stomach.

Juliana eyed the handsome pair of chestnuts harnessed to the curricle. High-steppers, Tommy would say. Granville's groom was holding them, and at the moment they looked calm enough. The thought of driving them, however, was daunting, and she wondered uneasily how stable the low-built curricle was.

Granville, whom she was beginning to suspect did not have any nerves whatsoever, greeted her warmly and helped her up. He took the reins in hand and motioned to the groom. The boy stepped away as one of the horses lifted his head, and then he scurried to climb up on the back of the vehicle. The earl controlled the pair easily enough and as they started off down the drive, Juliana relaxed a little. At least he didn't expect her to take the ribbons immediately, and his next words were reassuring.

"For now, I would like you to observe how I hold the reins and how they control the horses. Later, if you feel comfortable doing so, you may handle the ribbons yourself."

She nodded, watching his hands intently. He held the reins looped through his fingers.

"You need to be firm enough to let the horses know you are in control, but with a light enough touch so as not to damage their mouths. My horses are well trained and will respond readily. But if you jerk the reins, they'll fight you all the way."

Juliana kept her gaze on his fingers, and Granville, glancing at her, smiled. She was altogether too serious. "Horses are rather like females, Miss Chevron. Generally, they will respond to a light touch."

She looked up, about to object to the comparison, when she saw his smile. "It's hardly a complimentary likeness, sir."

"Ah, but it is. Most gentlemen prize their cattle above all else. To compare a young lady to this most valued possession must surely be thought an accolade of the highest order."

"I beg to differ with you. To be thought horse-faced or mulish is scarcely praise."

"Unfortunately, neither the horses nor women are all praiseworthy. You, however, would no doubt be termed a prime filly and a sweet-goer, which denotes an attractive young lady with an amiable disposition."

"I shall try to bear up under such fulsome compliments," she said, laughing.

Granville turned the team towards the west, and she noticed that although he held a whip in his hand, he never seemed to use it, and she enquired about its purpose.

"For style, mostly," he said, smiling. "Or if I am racing, a crack of the whip above the horses' ears will usually increase the pace, but I don't believe in whipping my team."

"I know," she said, a dimple appearing. "You believe in a light hand."

"Yes, Miss Chevron, and since you are such an apt pupil, I think it's time you tried your hand on the ribbons. Don't be nervous. Just place your hands over mine, and I'll thread the reins through your fingers."

It was a delicate business, but at last she was holding the reins, and as far as she could tell, the horses had not noticed the difference. She hoped they couldn't feel the tension running through her.

"Relax," Granville said, watching as she bit her lip. "The worst that can happen is they'll bolt, and I'm right here. Now then, gently pull the reins a fraction to the right. We're in the centre of the road. That's it. Wonderful!"

Juliana barely heard him, concentrating all her energy on holding the powerful team. It was a heady feeling, and she was almost enjoying herself when she saw the carriage rounding the bend and coming straight at them. "Granville!"

"I see it, Miss Chevron. There's nothing to be concerned about. Just hold them straight. Steady."

The carriage swept by and out of the corner of her eye she saw the driver lift a hand to the earl. He waved and she wanted to scream at him. They were approaching a turn in the road.

"You're doing fine. Just guide them round the bend. Pull gently to the right. A bit more—that's it. See, nothing to it."

If she could have, she would have glared at him but she was afraid to take her eyes off the road. Granville reached over and gently took the reins from her. "Enough, for now. You did splendidly for your first lesson."

Juliana sat back relieved, the tension draining from her. She had not realized how stiffly she'd been sitting, but she felt the strain across her shoulders and in her arms. Driving was certainly not as easy as it looked, and she watched with admiration the way Granville handled the ribbons so easily.

She hardly noticed as he turned off the main road, driving down a narrow lane. The going was difficult, the lane filled with deep ruts which Granville skilfully avoided. Juliana was thankful she wasn't driving, and breathed a sigh of relief as the earl pulled the horses up in front of a neat cottage. The sound of dozens of dogs barking assaulted her ears. Had he brought her to visit his kennels?

A wizened old man, leaning heavily on a cane, shuffled round the cottage as the earl was helping Juliana down. The man's long white beard contrasted sharply with his tan, leathery face. Small, bright blue eyes looked at Juliana curiously.

The earl turned, greeting the gnomelike man warmly. "Alf, how are you, old friend? I see you've the cane out. Is the leg troubling you?"

"Nought that I can't bear, my lord."

"I've brought you a visitor, Alf," he said, nodding at Juliana. "Miss Chevron is a protégée of my aunt's, and I think she may be able to help us with our problem."

"What problem you speaking of, my lord?" he asked, a trace of belligerence in the coarse voice.

"Getting you some help, Alf. Now do not begin to pucker up. I am *not* pensioning you off. I only want to arrange an assistant for you. A boy you might train to take over one day. When *you* are ready to retire. Is Sarah at home?"

"Aye," he mumbled almost rudely, and then turned to Juliana. "Would you like to step in, miss? The kettle will be on the boil and like as not Sarah will have some fresh baked bread to offer you."

Juliana smiled hesitantly and started to thank him, but Alf had already turned his back and was heading for the door. She followed, thinking him a strange creature, but secure in the knowledge that the earl was just a step behind her.

They were met at the door by a plump, tiny lady, her curly hair as white as Alf's.

"Gracious me, Lord Granville," she cried, wiping her hands on her apron and bobbing a curtsy all in one motion. "Why, it's been an age since you paid us a visit. And who is this pretty young lady?" Her brown eyes twinkled and she nudged her husband. "Don't be standing there like a great lump—get out the wine. We must have a drink, for it's not every day his lordship brings his young lady to call."

Juliana blushed under the woman's scrutiny, but Granville only laughed and presented her. "Pay Sarah no mind," he advised. "She's been trying to marry me off for years."

"The good Lord didn't intend for man to live alone," Sarah said, lifting a fat tabby off a handsomely carved chair. "Two by two is how they came on the ark, and how He intended we should live. Where do you think Alf would be without me to look after him?"

She whisked a basket of sewing off the sofa and invited Juliana to take a seat. Granville took the carved chair, clearly the seat of honour, but there was little room for him to stretch his long legs, and he looked decidedly out of place. If he was uncomfortable, he didn't show it, and ignoring Sarah's remarks, said tea and some of her baked bread would do fine.

"No wine, my lord? I've some special set aside, and it would be no trouble."

"Not today, Sarah. I've come to speak to you and Alf about taking on a lad to help with the kennels."

Sarah cast a worried look towards the kitchen. "I reckon he could use some help, but he's dead set against it. Ever since you mentioned retiring to him last year, he's been fretting you'll turn him off. It'd be the death of him if he couldn't work with the hounds."

"I know, Sarah. Trust me."

She nodded as Alf returned and the talk was desultory while Sarah served hot tea with thick, crusty slices of bread and creamy sweet butter. She sat next to Juliana, and even on the edge of the cushion, her short legs barely touched the floor. She urged the earl and Juliana to eat, but all the while her brown eyes watched her husband with a concern which touched Juliana's heart.

Granville set down his cup, refusing a refill, and came to the point. "Alf, there's a young lad I met, a friend of Miss Chevron's, and I'd like your help with him. He's a good boy, well mannered and intelligent. He has a way with dogs—nothing like your touch, of course—but he could be instructed, I think."

Alf sat with his gnarled hands folded on top of his cane and refused to meet the earl's eyes.

"He's only eight, but you always said a hound master should be trained young. I thought if he could come to you during the week, why then in ten or twenty years, he'd make a good assistant."

The old man looked up then, a spark of interest in his eyes. "Eight, you say?"

"He's the son of a carter, but has no interest in the business. His pa tells me he's always running off to tend to stray dogs. Seems a pity not to train him, but I know it'd be asking a lot of you and Sarah. Having a young boy underfoot all the time—"

"Got to teach 'em young. If they don't grow up with the hounds, it's no good. Got the touch, you say?"

Granville nodded. "He's done wonders with a mongrel he picked up. I sent Homer to him to show him a few pointers, but—"

"Humph. Better send him to me. That one don't know half what he thinks he does."

Sarah's plump cheeks puffed out as she chuckled. "A young boy in the house. Reckon I'd better start baking. I know how boys can eat. What's he like, my lord?"

"Ask Miss Chevron. She knows him better than I," Granville said, and settled back to listen while Sarah garnered every detail of young Willie's life. It was close to an hour before they could take their leave.

Juliana glanced back over her shoulder, waving once more to the tiny couple in the doorway. It was a wonderful opportunity for Willie, and Alf and Sarah seemed excited over having a young boy in the house. She had not wanted to dampen their enthusiasm, but she wondered what William would say, and voiced her doubts to Granville.

"I don't think he'll object. Willie will be apprenticed and his wages will go to his father until he's of age. If William needs more help in the yard, he'll be able to afford to hire a boy. In the meantime, his son will learn a good trade and eventually he'll take his place as Master of the Kennels."

She watched his profile in the late-afternoon light. He looked so aloof, almost arrogant, and yet he behaved with a great deal of kindness and understanding.

Sensing her gaze, he glanced at her, his brows lifting quizzically. "What now, Miss Chevron? Have I a spot on my nose?"

"No, my lord. Just a crack in your armour."

CHAPTER SIX

WITH A TWIST OF HER WRIST, Juliana tooled the curricle smartly down the lane leading towards Crowley. After two weeks of instruction from the earl, she was handling the team easily and with an air of confidence which Granville found diverting.

"You have improved vastly, Miss Chevron. No one would ever guess that only a few weeks ago, you had never driven a team."

"From you, sir, that is high praise, but I fear I will never be able to compete with The Fielding."

"For which I am devoutly thankful. One such lady driving recklessly through the Park is enough. I shudder to think what would happen if every young lady drove with her mad abandon. Someone would be certain to duplicate Cromwell's wild ride."

Secure enough now to glance up at him, Juliana did so, smiling. "Elucidate, sir. I sense one of your tall tales."

"A footnote in the pages of history, Miss Chevron," he corrected. "Never tell me you are ignorant of Oliver Cromwell's Hyde Park adventure?"

"I fear so, my lord, and to think I once believed myself well versed in history! You have depressed all my pretensions. Tell me this tale of Cromwell."

"'Tis written that the Lord High Protector of all England enjoyed driving his carriage and is said to have had an excessive fondness for the whip."

"Heavens, the foolish man is obviously headed for disaster. Did no one tell him to use a light hand on the reins?"

"Apparently not. On one occasion—"

"Perhaps his advisers were not of your calibre, my lord," she suggested gravely.

"On that one memorable occasion," the earl said, raising his voice, "he provoked his horses so much that they bolted. The postillions could not hold them and Cromwell was flung out of his carriage. He landed, most unfortunately on the pole, and got his foot somehow entangled in the trappings. The horses dragged him some distance, and a pistol he was carrying in his pocket was accidentally discharged. You can imagine the chaotic scene which ensued."

Juliana laughed. "You do know the oddest things, and it is a horrifying picture you paint, my lord, but I thought that driving in the manner of Lady Fielding was the object of these lessons."

"To handle a team capably is sufficient," he said, watching the way the light breeze lifted the curls from her cheek.

"Do you think so? Georgia says Lord Johnny admires The Fielding very much."

"My brother may admire her, as do many gentlemen, but he would never seek to wed her. No gentleman would wish to have a wife who behaves so notoriously."

"Now you sound like Georgia with her strictures on the preferences of gentlemen," she teased, glancing up at him.

"Keep your eyes on the road," he warned, seeing a carriage in the distance. There was very little traffic on the winding country lanes and Juliana had not had much practice passing other vehicles. He saw her tense slightly, biting her lip as she did when she was concentrating.

She tightened the reins slightly, slowing their carriage. "Someone is in a great hurry," she said, watching the cloud of dust approaching.

"A fool, by the way he is driving," Granville answered, no longer lounging at his ease. He was ready to take the reins if necessary, and silently cursed the man driving a high-perch phaeton and four on a country road as though it were the racecourse at Brighton.

Juliana continued to hold the team steady, confident of her ability to handle the chestnuts. All she need do was keep a firm hand on the reins and the carriage would give them the go-by.

Granville's attention was on the deep blue phaeton and four matched greys. There were not many such rigs in England, and he feared he knew the driver of this one. "Pull them up, Miss Chevron," he ordered, all trace of humour gone.

Juliana was loath to obey, but silently brought the chestnut team to a halt on the side of the road. She was prepared to hand over the reins, but Granville made no move to take them. He was intently watching the phaeton approaching, and she followed his gaze. Whatever she might think of the folly of driving so fast on such a road, she could not help but admire the gentleman's style. She had only a glimpse of him as he passed, a well-proportioned young man, with curling black locks above a handsome face.

The dashing driver cracked his whip as he passed them, barely glancing at the curricle. She saw Granville wave, and a moment later, the young man was reining in his horses. She watched with admiration as he turned them neatly in an impossibly narrow space, and came abreast of them again, carelessly blocking the road.

"Spence, old man! I was just on my way to see you. Fancy meeting you in the lane, and driven by a young lady, too. Well, well." He grinned down at them, strong white teeth showing clearly against a tanned face lit by a pair of laughing blue eyes.

Juliana, craning her neck to look up at him, couldn't help returning his infectious smile. She didn't need Granville to tell her that this was the infamous Madcap Johnny. There could not be two such bold gentlemen in England, not with that sort of devil-may-care look about him and broad, good-natured grin. The gossips had not done him justice, she thought and barely heard Granville answer him.

"Hello, Johnny. I hardly expected you back so soon. Did you take care of everything at Southwell?"

"So soon? It's been nearly a month, dear brother," Johnny said, without taking his glance off Juliana. "The stables are fine, but what have you been up to behind my back? Obviously, you've not been missing me."

"If you can contrive to turn that phaeton again, you may follow us back to Crowley, and I will introduce you properly to Miss Chevron."

"Nothing to it," the younger man boasted. Sweeping off his beaver, he managed to execute a neat bow to Juliana while holding in check four very high-strung

horses. "You must be an excellent whip for my brother
to trust you with his cattle. Do you race?"

"She does not," Granville answered firmly, and
motioned for Juliana to drive on.

She reluctantly lowered her head, dutifully giving the
horses the office to start, but could not resist glancing
back at Lord John. He waved jauntily as he turned his
horses, and moments later she heard the phaeton
coming up behind her. She shook the reins, urging the
horses on a bit. This was, after all, the gentleman who
admired The Fielding.

She turned into the avenue leading to Crowley and
heard Granville utter a curse. Juliana, glancing at him,
saw the reason for his distress. Lord John meant to
make a race of it and was moving the phaeton up
alongside the curricle.

Without thinking, she impulsively urged her team on
and felt a surge of exhilaration as they increased their
speed.

"Slow down, Miss Chevron," Granville cautioned.
"Pay John no heed. It scarcely matters if he reaches
Crowley before us."

She checked for an instant, but the sight of the greys
drawing abreast was too much for her good intentions, and she gave the chestnuts their head over
Granville's protests. They were Thoroughbreds, and
the sight and sound of a team of horses bearing down
on them brought out their racing instincts. They surged
forward, their awesome power unleashed. Too late,
Juliana realized she'd lost control.

The road curved just in front of the house, and the
chestnuts would have plunged straight ahead across the
lawn had not Granville seized the reins. He stood up,
exerting his will against the strength of the runaway

team. Hauling on the reins, his face straining with the effort, he fought against their strength. The horses slowed a fraction and Granville, pulling sharply on the ribbons, forced them to take the bend.

Johnny passed him on the turn with a wild yell, his own greys under taut control. He brought them to a plunging standstill and as soon as his tiger reached their heads, he leapt down with catlike grace.

"Well done, Spence," he called as Granville brought his own team to a steaming halt. The capes of his driving coat swirled round him as he crossed the drive. Johnny put a calming hand on the bridle of the wild-eyed chestnut, laughing up at his brother. "I thought for a moment that you were going straight across the lawn."

Granville didn't answer him, save for a frosty glare. He climbed down silently and then stretched up a hand for Juliana.

She sat with her head down, a mortifying flush staining her cheeks. She had behaved foolishly, stupidly, and she knew she deserved every ounce of Granville's wrath—but she could not meet his eyes.

"Miss Chevron?" he prompted.

Reluctantly, Juliana allowed him to hand her down. With her feet steady on the ground, she looked up at him, her green eyes reflecting her remorse. "I am sorry, my lord. I don't know what possessed me to—"

"My dear girl, never apologize to him," Johnny interrupted, with an impudent grin. "It only adds to his consequence. Take my advice and carry off your indiscretions with a high hand. Besides, if anyone was at fault, which I don't for a minute own, then it was myself."

Granville made a visible effort to control his temper. "You were at fault, John. You endangered Miss Chevron's life—"

"Nonsense, old man. How could she be in any danger with you beside her on the seat? I know your skill as a whip." He grinned at Juliana. "There's no one better with the ribbons than Spence. Drives to an inch. Why, once he—"

"We shall discuss this later," the earl interrupted firmly. "Miss Chevron, please tell my aunt that John is here. We shall join you in the drawing-room shortly."

She obeyed him instantly, and leaving both gentlemen standing in the drive, entered the house. She found Georgia in the small sitting-room, and barely giving that lady time to greet her, Juliana confessed her folly.

"It was terrible, Georgia," she concluded, twisting her gloves in her hands. "Granville has been so kind and not only did I disobey his instructions, but I put us both in danger. And he had to use such force to stop the chestnuts from bolting that I can only pray my carelessness has not resulted in damaging their mouths."

"Do not worry so, darling," Georgia murmured absently, laying aside her needlework. "So Johnny is here? We shall have to alter our plans slightly, but it may be to our advantage. Tell me, dearest, did Spencer scold you?"

"No. He barely said a word."

"Pity. Johnny would have defended you instantly, and as you know, darling, a gentleman who feels protective towards a young lady is halfway to being in love with her. Spencer cannot have been thinking clearly."

"No...no, ma'am," Juliana said, trying valiantly not to give in to a hysterical fit of giggles. She should have known Georgia would not see the matter in the same light.

"Gracious, Juliana," Georgia scolded, looking up and seeming to see her for the first time. "You are all windblown! Hurry up and change before my nephews join us. The blue dress, I think. Remember, it is Johnny's favourite colour."

JULIANA DID NOT RETURN to the sitting-room. She was still in her dressing gown when Georgia tapped on her door twenty minutes later. She poked her head round the door. "Oh, good, you are not dressed yet. I've spoken with Johnny and I think it would be well to change our plans. I will tell him and Spencer that the drive unsettled you and you are resting until dinner."

"It *did* unsettle me, but not to that extent. What are you planning, Georgia?"

"Johnny is most anxious to make your acquaintance, darling. You made quite an impression on him, and now we shall tease him a bit. It never pays to gratify a gentleman's whims too quickly, you know. If I could only contrive it, I would whisk you out of the house before dinner, but I fear it is too late to arrange anything now." With an air of bemusement, she sat on the edge of the bed, caressing Felix's silky ears.

Juliana, seated in a chair before her dressing table, looked at the older woman in the mirror. "You should have been a general in the army, planning battle strategies."

"Thank you, dearest. To be sure, I could have managed our affairs better than certain gentlemen who shall remain nameless. I remember a most diverting conversation I had with General von Blucher—"

"The Prussian general?" Juliana interrupted, eyes wide with awe. Was there nothing Georgia would not dare?

"Yes, darling, he was in London during the Victory Summer, and I chanced to meet him at some house or other. I do like to think our little talk was helpful to him during that messy affair at Waterloo. He did seem to have taken my advice . . . but that is neither here nor there. It is your strategy we must discuss."

Juliana smiled. "Do you really think I should avoid Lord John until dinner? It seems a trifle silly."

"Silly! Gracious, child, if that is how you think, it is well I am here to guide you. One of the first things you must remember about gentlemen is that they *always* want what they cannot have. At present, what Johnny wants is to meet you. Therefore, you will avoid him. He will appreciate you all the more for having been kept waiting. You must trust me in these matters, darling."

Juliana agreed to it, hiding a smile. She did not object to keeping Lord John waiting, however nonsensical she thought the charade. There was only one matter which really concerned her. She rose gracefully to see Georgia out, but at the door she detained her, laying a hand on her arm. "Georgia, was Lord Granville very upset? Do you not think I should go down and apologize to him?"

"Heavens no, child. Were you not attending? You will remain here till dinner. As for Spencer, do not give him another thought. If he was angry at all, it was with Johnny, and you may be very sure that scapegrace knows perfectly well how to get round him. He will have Spencer in good humour by dinner—you may depend on it."

Juliana hoped she was right, and after Georgia left, she lay down to rest. Her troubled thoughts, however, precluded any hope of napping. Granville had been excessively kind to her. Teaching her to drive and waltzing with her in the evenings might be to his own benefit. But bringing Willie to Alf as an apprentice was not part of their agreement, and twice they had driven over to see how the boy was doing. Granville had suggested the trips, knowing she was worried about Willie. Needlessly. The boy had turned into a miniature Alf, aping his every move. He had even gained a few pounds, thanks to Sarah plying him with cookies and cake at every opportunity.

And there were the commissions Granville had secured for William. Anna had sent her a letter by Willie. They had almost more business than William could handle, thanks to his lordship's recommending the carter to his friends. Anna's letter was full of her gratitude, and she had urged Juliana to be certain to convey their thanks.

She had tried to thank him, but Granville had brushed her gratitude aside. He *claimed* he was indebted to her for finding him a likely lad to train as kennel master. As for the business he had directed to William, he said his friends were much obliged to him. An honest, reliable carter was difficult to find.

Whatever he might say, Juliana was conscious that he had gone to a great deal of trouble on her behalf. She had repaid him by ignoring his instructions and behaving as foolishly as Willie might have done. She knew, whatever Georgia might say, that she had acquitted herself very badly. Lord John might win the earl back to good humour, but that did not exonerate her own behaviour. She owed Granville an apology, and until that duty was discharged, she could not rest easily.

Her decision made, Juliana rose and pulled the bell-rope for Dorcas. She ran a comb through her tangled curls and was already struggling into her dress when the maid arrived.

"I thought you was resting, miss."

"There's something I must attend to first, Dorcas," she said, turning her back to the maid. "Help me button this, please."

The young girl obliged, working the long row of buttons into the delicate loops which held them. "Lady Alynwick said you'd be resting till dinner, miss."

"I tried to, but I find I cannot rest until I've seen his lordship. Do you know where he is, Dorcas?"

"He's in the stables, miss," the maid replied. "First thing he must do was see to those horses of his."

Of course, Juliana thought, the earl was undoubtedly concerned over the damage she had wrought. She had a dreadful picture of him tending to one of the chestnuts, the poor horse's mouth swollen and bruised.

"Will there be anything else, miss?"

"What? Oh, no. Thank you, Dorcas. You may come back later to dress my hair for dinner."

Juliana, waiting until the maid had left the hall, opened her door softly. There was no one in the long hall. Walking softly towards the stairs, she paused, her hand on the banister. Soft, indistinct voices floated up from the drawing-room. Good. Georgia must still be sitting with Lord John.

She was down the stairs and crossing the marble hall before the footman realized she was there. He glanced round and would have come at once to open the door for her, but Juliana waved him back. Smiling prettily, she slipped out the door.

Her silk slippers were never intended for walks on the gravelled path which led to the stables. Juliana winced, treading on a particularly sharp pebble, and wished she had thought to change her shoes. Today seemed to be her day for foolish behaviour.

Alwyn, brushing down a mare in the paddock area, saw her approaching and hailed her eagerly. "Miss Chevron! Are you riding today, miss? I could get Ladyslipper ready in no time."

"No, but thank you, Alwyn. I am looking for his lordship. Have you seen him?"

The lad nodded, his smile disappearing, replaced by a sullen pout. "He's in there," he mumbled, gesturing towards the stables.

Juliana nodded. Well, she could see for herself how the chestnuts were, and then apologize to Granville. Swallowing hard, she squared her shoulders and walked through the open doors, wondering where Ian was. If he knew how she'd abused the horses today, she would certainly be in his black books. The thought did little to encourage her and she looked round hesitantly.

"He's down towards the back, miss," Alwyn said. He'd followed her in and was standing at the open door, watching her.

Feeling she had little choice, Juliana made her way carefully past the stalls. A few of the occupants nickered as she passed, but she had no treats to bestow, and she paused only to give Ladyslipper a pat on the neck. She saw him in the next-to-last stall, on the far side of one of the grey mares Lord John had driven, his back to her. He was crooning softly to the stallion, calming it, she guessed, and running his hand gently down the horse's foreleg.

She leaned against the lower half of the Dutch door. "My lord, I could not rest until I apologized for my behaviour this afternoon. It was extremely foolish of me to... to spring your horses."

He said nothing. Did not even look round, although his hand stilled on the horse's leg. She knew he was listening.

"Please forgive me, sir. I know it was reprehensible of me, particularly after you have been so kind. Is there anything I can do to make amends?"

"A kiss perhaps?" he drawled, standing up and brushing the black curls from his brow. His eyes full of mischief, he added, "I promise I would forgive you anything if—"

"It's you! Oh! You must know I thought you were the earl. How *could* you stand there listening to me when you knew I had mistaken you for your brother?"

"How could I not?" he asked, laughing softly. In two swift steps he was at the door, looking down at her.

His eyes were blue, bluer than Granville's, she thought irrationally. Bluer and warmer and full of tantalizing promises.

"Better make your apology to me, Fair Charmer. It would be wasted on Granville. But I... I would forgive a lass with blue-black hair and beguiling green eyes anything," he murmured, placing a gentle hand beneath her chin to lift her face.

She felt his warm breath on her cheek, saw the strong lines of his throat where his shirt was open and stood perfectly still. It was not till he lowered his head that she stepped back, laughing aloud.

It was not quite the reaction Johnny expected, but he was not in the least offended, and quizzed her. "I am delighted to afford you so much amusement, Miss Chevron."

"So you remember my name?" she teased.

"Of course," he said, leaning against the door, his eyes assessing her. "Could you ever doubt it? I would not forget such a vision of loveliness. You have the most bewitching eyes and lips like the softest red rose just opening to the morning kiss of dew."

Her trill of soft, amused laughter seemed to fill the stables, echoing back in the huge vastness.

Johnny, dark brows drawn together over puzzled eyes, watched her for a moment. He could not help admiring the long graceful line of her neck or the way she tilted her head when she laughed. He stepped back, a devilish gleam in his eyes, and with hands on his hips, he watched her, waiting. "If you are quite finished?"

"Oh, my lord, now I *do* owe you an apology." She smiled sweetly, adding, "Though you did promise to forgive me anything."

"For a price, Fair Charmer," he said, stepping close again. "If you—"

"No, no. Please do not start that nonsense again," she interrupted, holding up her hand. "I *am* sorry and it was rude of me to laugh, but you must own those lines were straight out of a penny romance."

"No, are they?" he asked, intrigued. "Well, I cannot be faulted for that—I never read the things."

"Of course not. How...how foolish of me when Granville said you were not literary," she said, barely managing to get the words out without laughing again. Seeing his puzzled look, she tried to explain. "It is just

the sort of thing the hero says when he meets the heroine, and then of course, she melts into his embrace."

He looked regretful. "You, I gather, are not that sort
of heroine?"

"I fear not, sir. I cannot believe *anyone* would suc-
cumb to such shameless flattery."

"Well, they do, and much more often than you
would think," he assured her, with a boyish swagger.
"I shall have to look into these romances. Obviously,
the fellow that pens them knows a thing or two. Where
can I find one?"

"Try your aunt," she suggested, amused. "I am
certain Georgia will have one or two at hand. Now,
pray excuse me. I was looking for Lord Granville."

"To apologize? There's really no need, you know.
His cattle are fine, and he has forgotten the entire
matter by now."

"I only wish I might believe so."

"Oh, you may take my word for it. Spence might
ride a trifle heavy now and then, but it never lasts long.
He says what he has to say and is done with it."

"I gather you have had a great deal of experience
along those lines?"

He nodded, rolling his eyes back and drawing a finger across his throat in the manner of an execution.
"He's hung me out to dry more times than I care to
remember."

Johnny unlatched the lower part of the door, stepping out. "Let me walk with you to the house," he
suggested, offering his arm.

Juliana was suddenly and acutely aware of the im-
propriety of being alone in the stable with him. It had
not seemed so improper when Lord John was on the
other side of the door. "To the gardens, perhaps. I am

supposed to be in my room resting." Remembering Georgia's instructions, she added, "I hope you will not feel obliged to mention my presence here to your aunt."

"Aunt Georgia? A lot she would care. She's a darling. My favourite aunt."

"Oh, do you have others? I thought—"

"No, only the one," he said laughingly, interrupting her. "But if I did, Aunt Georgia would still be my favourite."

"Are you never serious, sir?" Juliana asked, glancing round the huge stables. It was unnaturally quiet and she wondered where everyone was. There was no sign of Ian, and even Alwyn had disappeared. She thought she heard a movement in one of the stalls near the door, but when she looked she saw only Ladybird, an elderly grey brood mare, poking her nose over the door.

"Rarely," Johnny was saying. "I leave that to Spence. He's the fusty one in the family, almost as stiff rumped as our father, and very correct, too. Full of outdated notions of polite behaviour. Now *he* would probably take exception to your being out here with me."

"You are undoubtedly right, and I hope you will refrain from mentioning the matter to him, as well," she said, trying to keep her voice light.

"It shall be our secret, Fair Charmer," he promised, grinning as her eyes flashed up at him.

They passed through the door into the yard, leaving the barn in silence, save for the nickering of a mare. The earl stepped forward, soothing her automatically, his eyes still on the door. The mare nudged him, demanding attention.

"Easy, old girl. Ian will be along in a minute to see to you." *Old*. That was how Johnny saw him. Old and fusty and stiff rumped. His words had hurt. Hurt as much as Juliana's lighthearted agreement. He ran his hand down between the mare's velvety eyes. Perhaps the old girl was not the only one who should be put out to pasture.

CHAPTER SEVEN

JULIANA HESITATED at the door of the salon. She noticed Lord John standing near the fireplace and Georgia sitting on the low sofa, but there was no sign of Granville. She had enquired for him on returning to the house that afternoon, and was frustrated when the footman could only tell her that he had stepped out some time ago and had not yet returned.

"Ah, there she is at last," Johnny said, catching sight of her, and immediately crossed the room to her side. He bowed, whispering softly, "Fear not, Fair Charmer, our secret is safe," before leading her to Georgia, and demanding, "if you do not introduce me at once to this vision, I swear I shall go mad."

Juliana gravely curtsied, but peeped up at him, her eyes full of mischief. "I fear it is already too late to save you, my lord."

"Never say so," he protested, watching as she seated herself, and smoothed the lines of a very becoming green silk gown.

"But are you not the infamous Madcap Johnny, known the length and breadth of England for your mad, mad deeds?"

He grinned, unabashed. "Have you been talking to my esteemed brother? I promise you, I am not nearly so black as I am painted."

"It's true that his reputation does not do him justice," Granville agreed, strolling into the room, and placing a brotherly arm round Johnny's shoulders.

"There, you see. Thank you, Spence, old man—"

"Not at all," the earl interrupted, adding smoothly, "he is far worse than most people could ever imagine."

"Really, Spencer," Georgia said, intervening, "that is not at all kind of you, and you will give Juliana a misguided impression." She patted Juliana's hand. "Pay no attention to Spencer's droll humour, darling, and allow me to present my other nephew, Lord John Drayton. Johnny, this is Miss Juliana Chevron. She is the daughter of an old friend and I have the privilege of sponsoring her come-out in London."

"Juliana," he repeated, drawing out the syllables. "What a delightful name. May I say it suits you admirably, Miss Chevron, having a certain musical lilt to it." He cast a suspicious glance at his aunt. "It *is* her real name?"

"Johnny, you odious boy! Would I introduce you to her by that name were it not her own?"

"Yes," both her nephews answered at once, and with such conviction that they all laughed.

"Actually, it is an honour to be rechristened by my aunt," Johnny said, making amends. "She only renames those people whom she likes."

"Or persons with impossibly unsuitable names," Georgia added scrupulously. "Juliana, however, is her own given name."

"Wasn't there a goddess or something by that name?" Johnny asked, his eyes on Juliana.

"I do not know, sir," she said, smiling. "I was named in honour of my grandfather, Jules."

"It seems to me there was—you know, like Aphrodite or one of those goddesses Byron or someone is always writing sonnets to."

"I do not believe so," Granville answered, taking his usual chair. "Unless you are thinking of a saint—there were several Saint Julians, but then I can hardly think of Miss Chevron as saintly." He directed a small, ironical smile in her direction, before addressing his brother again. "Turning literary on us, Johnny?"

"I do believe he is, Spencer," Georgia said, laughing. "Can you imagine, your brother was asking me for the loan of a book this afternoon." Seeing his startled expression, she added, "I swear it is true."

Juliana smothered a laugh, but her glance was drawn to Johnny, who had the grace to look slightly embarrassed.

Georgia, seeing the look which passed between them, was well pleased. Her plans were progressing beautifully. There was an air of intimacy between the pair already. Wondering if Spencer had noticed, she glanced at him, but he had risen and was pouring a glass of sherry. Georgia thought fleetingly that he looked a trifle drawn. She said nothing, however, and beyond wishing he would not work so hard, returned her attention to Juliana.

DINNER WAS a lengthy affair, and if Granville was unnaturally quiet, Johnny made up for it with his high good spirits. They were lingering over dessert when Georgia brought up the affair of Percy Cochrane, demanding to hear the tale firsthand.

Johnny, much to his credit, made light of the story, telling it with a comical air, and making out his part to be more of a drunken buffoon than that of a hero.

Georgia would not have it, and protested, "Of course it was very wrong of you, Johnny, and I do not deny that, but Percy Cochrane deserved a come-uppance. Has done for years, in fact. I, for one, am very glad to know that he finally received it at your hands."

"I hope you still feel the same when Percy takes his revenge," Granville said without thinking.

Georgia's eyes widened, reflecting her concern. "You do not actually think Percy would try to harm Johnny?"

"Not physically, at any rate," the earl answered, immediately sorry that he had frightened the ladies. "Percy will do what damage he may with his tongue."

"If that is all, then we need not worry. No one who matters will pay the least attention to that vulgar little man."

"He would not be so foolish as to say anything directly, Aunt. No, he will work through his minions, spreading whispers wherever he can. I do not wish to alarm you, but you should be on your guard, and take care to avoid him in Town."

Johnny, for one brief instant, looked serious. "I never should have provoked him. *You* would have chopped him down neatly with a few well-chosen words, and given him the cut direct. And everyone would have followed your lead. I wish you'd been there, Spence."

"Perhaps, but the end result would still be the same."

"I do not wish to hear any more of this," Georgia declared, rising. "I will not allow that odious mushroom to spoil Juliana's Season. Come, dearest, let us retire to the salon. My nephews may join us when they have finished their discussion and their port.''

Georgia, master strategist that she was, directed Juliana to take her place at the harpsichord and arranged the sheet music for her. Every song which Johnny had ever mentioned being partial to, every tune he had ever hummed, was in Juliana's repertoire. Georgia even thought to place the sad, haunting ballads at the beginning, and the merrier tunes towards the back of the stand. That way the evening would end on a gay note.

She stepped back, observing the effect, and then moved a candelabrum nearer. The light fell softly on Juliana's face, highlighting her black curls.

''There, that is perfect. No one could help admiring the picture you present, darling. You look quite charming—but why didn't you wear the blue gown? Well, I daresay it does not matter. Green becomes you vastly, too, and brings out the colour of your eyes.''

That was what Granville had said, Juliana thought, idly striking a few keys. It was with him in mind that she had chosen the green gown. The neckline was not quite as revealing as the blue satin Georgia admired, though Juliana still thought it indecently low.

''Do not frown so, my dear. You know it creases your brow and causes wrinkles which may become permanent. Is something troubling you, child? If it is that business with Percy Cochrane, I beg you not to trouble your head over it. Spencer and Johnny between them are more than capable of dealing with *him*.''

''It's nothing,'' Juliana demurred, quickly summoning a smile. ''I think the wine made me a trifle melancholy.'' Her hands fingered the keys softly and she began singing a haunting, sweet song of a young girl's lost love, which fit her mood. Her voice was not trained, and did not carry far, but it was sufficient for the small salon.

Georgia sat down at the far end of the room, admiring the tableau she'd arranged, and listening with pleasure to the clear, true notes of her protégée's voice.

She was not alone in her enjoyment. Spencer and Johnny, electing to forgo their port in favour of the ladies' company, waited at the door. Not wishing to interrupt the ballad, they stood listening silently and applauded vigorously when the last note died away.

"Well done, Miss Chevron," the earl said enthusiastically and, strolling in, took the chair next to his aunt.

Johnny went straight to Juliana's side. "Well done, indeed. Will you give us another? I'll turn the pages for you, if you like."

She nodded her agreement and played a few notes. Johnny smiled widely, recognizing a merry soldier's tune. He hummed along with her, and then joined in the chorus.

"Old Bonaparte, he lost his heart,
When he saw a sea of Englishmen,
One look at the red, and then he fled,
We won't be seeing 'im again!"

Georgia smiled. What Johnny lacked in vocal accomplishment, he made up for in enthusiasm. What a divine couple they make, she thought, seeing his dark head bent towards Juliana. She had never seen Johnny so attentive to a young lady before. Of course, there were no other young ladies present to distract him. The thought gave her pause and she turned to Spencer impulsively. "Perhaps we should change our plans and remain at Crowley. It would provide Johnny a chance to further his acquaintance with Juliana, don't you think?"

"No!" He spoke more emphatically than he had intended, and was conscious of the curious way his aunt was regarding him. He laughed lightly. "I think such an idea would be fatal. You cannot have thought it through. Johnny would have no competition here. You know him—he would soon become bored. Much better to take her up to Town tomorrow as we planned. She is sure to be popular with the younger set, and there is nothing like a little jealousy to inflame a man."

"There is that, certainly," Georgia agreed, watching the couple at the harpsichord, her mind working rapidly. "But will Johnny come? He was speaking about dropping in on Somerset."

"I shall ask him to escort you and Juliana to Town, in my stead. I have some work which will keep me here for a few days yet. I think Johnny will not refuse me so simple and pleasurable a favour."

JULIANA TAPPED SOFTLY on the library door later that evening. She was determined to see Granville alone for a few minutes. He had left them as soon as she'd finished performing—not even joining them for tea. He'd pleaded the press of paperwork, but Juliana had the uncomfortable feeling he was avoiding her.

"Come in," Spencer called, hurriedly scattering papers across his desk, and bending his head as though engrossed in work. The last thing he wanted was a chat with Johnny.

"Forgive me for interrupting you, my lord," Juliana said from the door.

"Oh, it's you, Miss Chevron," he said, hastily rising. "I rather thought you were my brother. You should be asleep, my dear. You have a long day in front of you tomorrow." He knew he was rambling, saying whatever came into his head. She looked absurdly vulnerable standing there in the candlelight, as though she'd lost her best friend.

"I know, but I could not sleep yet and I...I was looking for Felix."

"He's in here, sound asleep, I'm afraid." He pointed towards the rug at the side of his desk. The spaniel was curled up in a contented ball, his furry coat moving rhythmically as he breathed deeply.

Juliana came as far as the desk, twisting her hands together. She spared only a glance for Felix. "It would seem a shame to disturb him now," she murmured, slipping into the large wing chair.

"You may leave him in here, if you like."

"Georgia said it would not be fair of me to take him to London. She says we will never be at home..."

"Are you worried about the pup, Miss Chevron? If that is all that is troubling you, please put it from your mind. I assure you I will take good care of him. I've become rather fond of the scamp."

"I know you would, my lord. That does not worry me."

"What is it then, my dear?" He sat down heavily, resisting the impulse to cross round the desk and comfort her. He knew it was highly improper for her to be alone with him, and equally improper of him to wish to keep her here.

"Georgia said you will not be accompanying us tomorrow, and I . . . I could not leave without apologizing, sir. I realize my behaviour this afternoon must have given you a disgust of me, but—"

"Now what have I said to make you think such a thing?" he demanded lightly, manufacturing a smile for her benefit.

"You have hardly said a word to me since," she answered honestly, watching his eyes. "During dinner, you were so quiet and afterwards in the salon . . . you left us as soon as I had finished playing."

"What a little egotist you are!" he declared, laughing. "I admit that just at present I am preoccupied with my work, Miss Chevron, but had I known you were imagining me to be merely sulking, I—"

"Oh, no! Not sulking, my lord," she interrupted, adding lamely, "I am sorry. I did not mean to imply that you would be solely concerned with me, and of course it must seem conceited in me to think so, but—"

"Come, Miss Chevron, what has happened to your delightful sense of humour? I was only teasing you. I assure you that though you may have acted impulsively this afternoon, it was the sort of thing anyone might have done, and I do not hold it against you—though I do hope you will not be tempted to try that sort of thing in London. You must remember poor Cromwell."

That brought a smile to her lips, and somewhat reassured, she rose. "Thank you, then, my lord. You have been most kind to me, and I just wanted you to know that . . . that I do appreciate it, and I shall miss you in Town."

He stood, determined to end this interview before he completely forgot himself. "Good night, Miss Chevron. You may leave with a light heart. I promise I shall take care of Felix for you, and I do not mean to desert you entirely in London. Doubtless you will be far too busy to notice, but I shall join you in Town in a few days."

Juliana nodded, and without another word left the library. She paused for a moment, leaning against the door. She felt she had somehow made a fool of herself. Regretting her decision to seek out the earl, she returned to her room as quietly as possible.

When Juliana was safe in her bedchamber, Georgia closed her own door softly. She had seen Juliana go into the library earlier. She owned she should not have allowed it. No proper chaperone would, but propriety was such a bore sometimes and the girl would come to no harm with Spencer. Had it been Johnny... but that was not the case. What had the child wanted with Spencer? They had both behaved a trifle strangely during the evening. Pulling the bellrope for her maid, Georgia sat down in front of the mirror, her mind busy with speculation.

It was some time before either of the ladies slept.

THE MORNING DAWNED clear and bright. By the time breakfast was finished, the fourgon had been packed and already dispatched to Georgia's town house in London, and the travelling chaise waited in the drive below. Juliana, glancing out her bedchamber window, was tempted to stick her tongue out at the impudent sun. She was as loath to leave Crowley as she'd been to arrive, and the fine, summery day seemed to mock her feelings.

Dorcas tapped lightly on the door and poked her head in. "Are you ready, miss? Her ladyship is downstairs waitin' on you."

Felix, seeing the open door, dodged round the maid, running to Juliana's side. He sat happily before her, head cocked, his large, dark eyes looking up at her hopefully.

Juliana swiftly knelt, caressing the silky ears. "You be a good boy, Felix, and look after his lordship," she whispered softly, feeling a trifle ridiculous for the lump in her throat.

Dorcas, waiting patiently by the door, coughed discreetly.

Juliana rose, smiling foolishly. "I shall miss this little fellow, you know." She picked up her gloves and reticule, withdrawing a pound note from its silk-lined pocket. "And you, too, Dorcas. Thank you very much for your care of me," she said, pressing the vail into the girl's hands.

"Oh, miss, thank you! All of us here are right sad to see you leaving, miss, and we hope you'll be coming back again before long."

"I hope so, too, Dorcas," she replied, with a last glance round the room, now restored to its former pristine orderliness. Save for Felix, there was nothing to indicate she'd ever occupied the chamber. "Come on, fellow. You can see us off."

Lady Alynwick was waiting in the Great Hall, and glanced up as Juliana descended the stairs. "There you are, darling. We must hurry. You know how gentlemen hate to keep their horses standing, though I confess I do not understand how it could possibly hurt them on such a beautiful morning. It is not as though they were exerting themselves in any way, is it?"

"No indeed, ma'am," she agreed, smiling, and crossed the room to make her goodbyes. There was a flurry of leave-taking, and she pressed generous tips on the housekeeper and butler. Piedmore, whom she'd once thought so formidable, smiled benignly, wishing her a safe journey. Mrs. Jamison, sniffing audibly, said it had been so very nice having miss in the house, and hoped she'd have the pleasure of another visit soon.

Juliana nodded, not trusting her voice, and followed Georgia out. Lord John was waiting on the steps, chatting idly with his brother. Granville's back was to them, but he turned as Johnny hailed them.

Georgia hugged Spencer, accepted his chaste salute on her cheek, and demanded Johnny's arm to the carriage.

"Well, Miss Chevron, your adventure is about to begin," Granville said, extending his arm. "I wish you Godspeed and good fortune."

"Thank you, my lord," she murmured, allowing him to place her hand in the crook of his arm as they strolled towards the carriage. "You will join us in London soon, will you not?"

"In a few days, perhaps, but judging by the start you have made, I doubt you will have need of me." He gestured towards his brother, mounting a handsome roan stallion. "Johnny is near captivated. If you need advice, let yourself be guided by my aunt. Beneath her frivolous chatter, she is a very shrewd lady."

They were near the carriage, and she only nodded as he handed her in. He put up the steps himself, securely shutting the door. Juliana watched him out the window, but there was no time to say anything more. He stepped back, giving a wave to Johnny, and the carriage rolled forward. Her last glimpse of him was standing on the steps of Crowley, Felix prancing at his heels.

THEY ARRIVED at Grosvenor Square late in the afternoon. No sooner had the footman let down the steps than Grim was there to assist Lady Alynwick. He had been on the watch for her since their baggage had arrived earlier, and a refreshing tea was laid out and waiting for them in the Oriental Room.

Georgia signalled her approval, but insisted on showing Juliana to her room personally, a mark of favour which was not lost on any of the servants. It was a large corner room near the back of the house, and partially shaded from the sun by a large, graceful oak. The chamber was tastefully decorated in bright colours with a yellow rose motif. The effect was delightful, and Juliana evinced some surprise.

"I save the dragons and crocodiles for the sitting-room, my pet," Georgia said, laughing at her expression. "Now, hurry and change. We shall have tea and discuss our plans. Milly will bring you down when you are ready," she added, indicating a petite brunette standing respectfully near the wardrobe.

Milly proved far more competent than Dorcas, but Juliana missed the latter's ingenuous chatter. Milly helped her into a pretty blue-and-white-striped silk day dress, without comment, and then offered to brush her hair. Juliana consented, trying to draw the girl out.

"Have you been in service here long, Milly?"

"No, miss."

"Well, I am sure you must be happy here. Lady Alynwick is a wonderful person."

"Yes, miss," she answered, stepping back respectfully. "Shall I show you down now?"

Juliana agreed, following her down the hall. The house was a large one, as were most of them on the north side of Grosvenor Square, and tastefully decorated by Georgia. None of the rooms she glimpsed were done up as extravagantly as the Oriental Room. All were painted or papered in pale hues, furnished with soft rugs, comfortable furniture and attractive paintings. It was only in her private sitting-room that Georgia gave rein to her more extravagant side. Stepping into the exotic room was a little like entering another world.

"Come in, my dear," Georgia called. "Grim has provided us with a delightful tea, and we may have a comfortable cose. Did you find everything you needed?"

"Yes, thank you," she murmured, sitting down opposite Georgia, and glancing round the room. "While I am glad not to be sleeping beneath fire-breathing dragons, I must say this room grows on one."

"Do you truly like it? You are not saying so merely to be polite, are you? I will tell you Spencer thinks it quite garish."

"And Lord John?" Juliana asked.

"Let me see if I can recall how he phrased it," Georgia said, her eyes twinkling as she handed Juliana one of the delicate blue-and-white teacups. "The first time Johnny saw it was in the spring of last year. We had just returned to Town and it was one of those dreary, grey days and rather chilly. Grim had the fire lit in here and the curtains drawn against the cold. He showed Johnny in and my nephew, not seeing me at my desk, said to him, 'Egad, this must be what a brothel in hell looks like. Flaming hot and not a wench in sight.'"

"Oh, no!" Juliana laughed, picturing the scene. "He must have been mortified when he saw you."

"Not Johnny. I rose from my desk and upon seeing me, he turned to Grim and said very cooly, 'I beg pardon, Grim. My eyes deceived me, but I see now this must be a heavenly abode for there is an angel in the corner there.'"

"Your nephew has a silvery tongue, Georgia."

"If you mean Johnny, yes. Compliments fall from his lips as profusely as raindrops from a cloud. It is as natural to him as breathing, and sometimes I think he is hardly conscious of what he says. Spencer is the reverse of the coin. His address is adequate, charming even—when he pleases—but he hoards his compliments, doling them out like a miser."

"You mean he does not merely pay lip-service?" Juliana asked, smiling. "I agree, but perhaps... perhaps his praise means all the more for not being so freely given." She gestured helplessly, not quite sure how to express what she meant.

"Somewhat akin to dieting, do you mean?" Georgia asked, helping herself to a slice of lemon cake. "If one does not allow one's self to have any cake for a month, then it will taste all the sweeter at the end for being a rare treat."

"Something like that." Juliana laughed, accepting the proffered dish of cake. "Was that what you were thinking of when you delayed my meeting with Lord John?"

Georgia nodded, but her attention was distracted. Grim was at the door. "Lord John and Lord Guilford are calling, my lady."

"Oh, how delightful. Show them in," she said, rising gracefully, and when Grim had withdrawn, she whispered. "I have been away a month—now I shall have my cake."

Juliana stood watching as she swept forward to greet her nephew. Johnny received a quick kiss and was released. He strode to Juliana's side while Georgia gave both her hands to Lord Guilford. He was an older man and towered over the diminutive Georgia. His full head of white hair proclaimed his age, but he had the build and vigour of a much younger man. Cake indeed, Juliana thought, watching them.

"Clever of me, was it not?" Johnny whispered, bowing over Juliana's hand. "I brought Guilford along to distract my aunt. He's been a beau of hers for years."

She had no chance to answer him, and would not have known what to say. Smiling boyishly, his eyes dancing with mischief, he was impossible to rebuke.

Then Georgia, her hand still clasped in Guilford's, was there, and introductions were made before the four settled down. The ladies sat on the low sofa, Lord Guilford drawing his chair close to Georgia, and Johnny moving a wing chair to Juliana's side. Georgia rang for fresh tea and, looking unusually flushed, poured out for Lord Guilford. Almost as an afterthought, she handed Johnny a cup.

As a chaperone, Georgia was less than adequate. All her attention was focused on Lord Guilford and Juliana could have left the room with Johnny without her ever noticing.

"We decided we could not allow two such lovely ladies to spend their first night in Town alone," Johnny said, claiming her attention. "They're putting on *The Merchant of Venice* at Drury Lane, or if the theatre is not to your taste, we could all go to Vauxhall Gardens."

"How kind of you," Juliana said, "but it is up to your aunt, and I believed she planned a quiet evening at home."

"Even better. She's certain to invite us to dine, and no one sets a better table than my aunt. I told Hadley not to expect me home for dinner."

"You are sure of your welcome, my lord."

"Not mine—Guilford's," he said in a low voice. "He and my aunt were sweethearts once, you know. He'd not come into the title then, and was in a line regiment. Aunt Georgia wrote to him faithfully and they were to be married when he came home. Then Charles was reported missing in action. She waited three years but there was no word of him and she finally married my uncle. Poor Charles came home six months later."

"Oh, how terrible. She must have felt dreadful."

"No doubt. My Uncle Halbert was not a joy to live with. Oh, I see, you mean about Guilford. Well, rather, but what could she do? She's not the sort of lady to have an . . . uh, that is, she was ever faithful to my uncle. Remained with the old codger right to the end."

"And Lord Guilford?" Juliana asked, stealing a glance at the handsome older man.

"Well, I was still in small clothes at the time, but the story goes he married a year later to please his mother and beget an heir. Star-crossed lovers. His wife almost died in childbirth, and the babe was stillborn. Ironic, is it not? Marriage is a risky business. Just shows you the dangers of rushing into it."

She hid the smile at his dour look, and prompted him. "And now?"

"Now?" he asked, with a puzzled air, reaching for a strawberry pastry.

Juliana lightly tapped his fingers with her fan. "Not another bite, my lord, until you finish this tale."

"It's a delicate affair, this. Perhaps we should stroll in the garden and I could whisper it in your ear. Did anyone ever tell you your ears are like seashells?"

Her gurgle of laughter stopped his foolishness, and he grinned good-naturedly. "Oh, very well. Guilford's wife was invalidish after the babe died and he took her off to live in the country. No one saw much of them, and I heard she finally died a few years ago. Guilford went abroad for a while. I believe he's only been back for a few months."

"A romantic tale, sir," Juliana said, rewarding him with the pastry he was eyeing.

"You *could* call me Johnny," he suggested. "After all, we are practically related."

Juliana's lips quivered, but she answered gravely, "How indeed, my lord?"

"Well, you are my aunt's protégée, so doesn't that make us cousins or something?"

"No, my lord, it certainly does not."

"Juliana," Georgia interrupted, rising. "Lord Guilford has suggested we might enjoy a drive in the Park. Would you care for it?"

"It sounds delightful, and normally I should like it above all things, but I am rather tired from the drive this morning. Would you object if I remained here and rest a bit?"

"No, darling, of course not," Georgia assured her, not at all displeased. "And you, Johnny?"

He could not stay—the dictates of polite behaviour would not allow it, nor did he wish to act as chaperon for his aunt. "I think I'll just stroll round to Boodle's, and see who's in Town, but I'll look in on you later, if I may?"

Georgia nodded, her mind elsewhere. She looked as excited as a schoolroom miss going out for her first drive. She excused herself and hurried off to fetch her hat and gloves. Lord Guilford, looking rather dazed himself, strolled across the room and stepped out into the garden. It was left to Juliana to see Lord John out.

"Are you really that tired, Juliana?" Johnny asked softly as they stood near the door.

"No," she said, laughing up at him. "But after that tale of yours, how could I intrude on Georgia? She deserves some time alone with her beau."

"And what of me?" he asked in the stillness of the hall. He leaned close to her. "Do I not deserve something for bringing him round? One small cousinly kiss?"

"Your hat, my lord," Grim said, stepping out into the hall, and bowing smoothly, his face impassive.

Juliana stepped back, her eyes full of amusement, her manner formal as she extended her hand. "Good afternoon, my lord. I shall look forward to seeing you later this evening."

"You'd think my aunt would employ a butler with more discretion," he complained in a loud whisper, bowing over her hand. After setting his hat at a jaunty angle, he nodded to her. "It was unfortunate we were interrupted earlier, Miss Chevron, but I promise you I shall continue our conversation later."

CHAPTER EIGHT

TWO DAYS LATER, Juliana made her bow to London Society at a small, very select party given by Lady Ursula Spalding. As Georgia predicted, Juliana was an instant success—at least with the gentlemen. Of course, arriving on the arm of Lord John had not hurt. She had the immediate attention of everyone in the long drawing-room. And while one or two cattish matrons were heard making waspish comments on the new beauty's advanced age, most had been pleased with her arrival.

Lady Carew was heard to remark to Mrs. Sidney that perhaps now her Claudia would give over mooning after Lord John and turn her attention to Roland Tilbury. Mrs. Sidney had nodded knowingly. Her own daughter had turned down two exceptionally suitable offers during the last Season, and all because that dashing young man had stood up with her on three different occasions. She watched Lord John as he handed Miss Chevron a glass of lemonade, and could almost sympathize with her daughter. The sooner that handsome scoundrel was taken out of circulation, the better it would be for everyone.

Miss Carew and Miss Sidney did not share their mamas' opinions, and looked with less than favour on Miss Chevron,. Not only had that damsel managed to secure Lord John's escort, but the other gentlemen were all clamouring for her attention. The young ladies were prepared to be civil to her, but no more.

Miss Ruth Taunton, watching from a settee at the far end of the room, noted the chill of their greetings and smiled at such foolishness. She managed to catch Lord John's attention, gesturing for him to bring Miss Chevron to her. *She* cherished no romantical notions about Lord John, or any other gentleman, for that matter. She watched Juliana crossing the room at his side, admiring the graceful way she moved. Then Johnny was bending over her hand.

"Ruth, I barely had a chance to say hello earlier. How are you?" he asked, his blue eyes losing their gaiety for a moment, as he regarded the girl with an air of unusual concern.

"Perfectly well, except that I am dying of thirst in this overheated room. Would you be a darling and fetch me something cool to drink?" she pleaded, and then smiled up at Juliana. "Miss Chevron, will you join me for a few minutes?"

"Thank you," Juliana murmured, sitting down next to her. "It is rather warm," she said politely while covertly studying the petite girl beside her.

"At least in this corner of the room. I thought you were finding it a trifle chilly over there," Ruth said softly, a question in her bright hazel eyes.

"I do seem to be regarded with a certain cool reserve," Juliana admitted, watching the young girls across the room glancing at her from behind their fans.

"You are not surprised, are you? Waltzing in here on Johnny's arm was certain to incur you the resentment of almost every young lady in the room."

"Excepting yourself, Miss Taunton?" Juliana asked. There was something curious here. Ruth Taunton had a delicate, almost translucent complexion, large deep-set eyes, and long, dark auburn hair. What was she doing hidden away in this quiet corner?

"Oh, I do not count. Johnny is a very dear friend and nothing could make me happier than to see him finally fall in love," she said, glancing at Juliana, her lips curving in a smile. "*Is* there a match in the making? I should dearly love to be the first to know."

"Then I shall promise to tell you... if there is ever anything to tell. Now, explain why you are sitting here all by yourself? If Lord John does not attract you, then surely one of the other gentlemen here must meet with your approval."

A slight blush delicately coloured Ruth's cheeks, but she smiled determinedly and met Juliana's eyes directly. "Did John not tell you? No, I suppose not. I am lame, Miss Chevron."

Juliana could not help looking down at the folds of the primrose gown covering Miss Taunton's limbs, if only for a brief second.

Ruth laughed lightly, but it had a forced sound, and her voice was strained as she answered, "Now I have made you uncomfortable and must apologize. You see why everyone avoids me."

"No... I mean, even if you *are* lame, surely you are not contagious?"

This time Ruth's laugh was natural, and her eyes warmed as she reached out for Juliana's hand. "Thank you. I hope we may be friends. I do get so tired of the pitying looks and I fear it sometimes makes me irritable."

"Well, I am sorry if your infirmity prevents you from dancing and being quite comfortable, but really

I could not pity anyone as beautiful as you are. Pray do not tell me that all the gentlemen are blind?"

"Oh, it is such a pleasure to talk with you. Do call me Ruth. As for the gentlemen—" She broke off, giving a careless shrug. "I make them uneasy. They do not quite know how to treat me. Even Johnny, whom I adore. Did you notice how he suddenly looked so serious when he greeted me? I would give anything to be treated just as the other girls are."

"Then we shall have to see what can be done," Juliana whispered as Johnny approached with Ruth's lemonade.

She saw at once what Miss Taunton meant. Johnny handed her the lemonade, moved a small table closer to the girl's hand and in a hushed voice asked if she were quite comfortable. He treated her as though she were quite sickly when anyone with an ounce of sense could see the excellent colour in her cheeks. Ruth thanked him pleasantly and then glanced at her new friend, her eyes full of amusement.

She didn't need to say a word. Juliana understood perfectly and could have cheerfully strangled Lord John. Instead, she gave him a pretty smile, inviting softly, "Do draw up a chair and join us, my lord. I was just explaining to Ruth the rules of a game we used to play at the Stapleton's. It's called Imagination, and is really quite easy." She glanced across the room and, seeing George Somerset listening with a bored expression to Miss Sidney, added, "If you would fetch your friend Mr. Somerset to join us, I could show you all how to play."

Lord John regarded her curiously but obligingly bowed and went off to summon George.

"Juliana!" Ruth protested. "What are you doing? Please don't think you need to sit here and amuse me."

"I suppose you think I'd rather be across the room listening to Miss Sidney and Miss Carew flattering Lord John? I promise you this will be a great deal more fun."

Ruth could not argue as the gentlemen approached and drew up their chairs, and in truth she was enjoying herself too much to protest too strongly. She listened carefully as Juliana outlined the rules of the game. It seemed absurdly simple. One person would begin and imagine an item beginning with the first letter of the alphabet. The next had to describe it in two or three words beginning with the next letter of the alphabet. The third had to describe it again but his last word had to rhyme with the item mentioned by the first player. The fourth player completed the stanza, rhyming his last word with that of the second player.

It sounded complicated to George Somerset, and the young blond giant shook his head. "I don't know, Miss Chevron. I'm not much in the way of word games."

"It doesn't matter, sir. Just say what comes to mind, but you must think fast, or you'll be ruled out. Now I'll begin."

"Oh, no you don't," Lord John protested. "The first player has it the easiest, and you've already played. Let Ruth begin."

"Not I," she said, laughing. "I like a challenge and fancy I am rather good at rhymes. I'll go last. You start, Mr. Somerset."

"All right then, but I warned you. Now, let's see. All right. I imagine an . . . army camp."

"Bleak as night," Juliana said quickly.

"Crowded and, er, damp," Johnny shouted, laughing.

"Desperate to fight," Ruth ended, ready with the rhyme. "But, Johnny—crowded and *damp?* What an image. At least Byron will not have to worry should you turn poet."

They all teased him, but he just grinned and George started them off with another round. It wasn't long before their shouts of laughter attracted the attention of the other young people in the room. Phillip Norwich, a dark-haired young man just down from Oxford, was the first to desert Miss Carew and Miss Sidney, and his friend Edward Hastings soon trailed after him. Harriet Malvern, Louise Holt and Olivia Pembroke strolled over together and the gentlemen fetched chairs for them. The rules were explained again and the rhymes extended. They became more ridiculous as the descriptions grew and the sounds of their merriment could be heard even in the card room down the hall.

Lady Spalding, looking into the room a few minutes later, laughed softly. She hurried back to the card room and explained to Georgia, "It is nothing to be concerned about. Your protégée has organized some sort of nonsensical word game and most of the young people are playing."

"I am relieved to hear it," Georgia commented dryly. "Now tell me why you are looking so smug."

"Oh, dear, am I?"

"Ursula, you could not look more pleased if the Prince Regent had strolled in. Is it Juliana? What mischief is she brewing?"

"She is a darling girl and I will not hear a word against her. Georgia, she has somehow managed to get my niece involved. For once, Ruth seems to be the centre of attention—and Claudia and Blanche are sitting by themselves at the other end of the room, with only poor Roland Tilbury to dance attendance on them!''

Georgia smiled. She knew how hard Ursula had tried to draw Ruth out of her shell. She was a charming girl but so self-conscious of her lameness that she could rarely be persuaded to attend any outing, and none at all if dancing was involved. Georgia was not sorry Juliana had befriended her—she only wished that it had not been at the expense of Claudia Carew. She would make trouble for Juliana if she could, and her cousin Percy would be only too glad to help her.

LADY ALYNWICK, who had fully intended to warn Juliana against the danger of antagonizing Miss Carew, forgot to mention the matter. Indeed, she forgot a number of things as Lord Guilford's visits to Grosvenor Square occurred with increasing frequency in the days following the rout. Not only was he her escort for whatever parties they attended in the evenings, but he called each afternoon with new plans for her amusement. He said on Monday that he thought she and Miss Chevron might enjoy a visit to Mrs. Salmon's Waxworks in Fleet Street—a treat Juliana hastily declined in favour of a drive to the Bayswater Tea Gardens.

"Lord John and Mr. Somerset are shooting in an archery tournament there, Georgia, and Lady Spalding said she would go with Ruth and me if you did not object."

Georgia did not object, and Juliana, strolling with Johnny in the Tea Gardens later that afternoon, confided to him, "She just said, 'Of course, darling,' and then told Lord Guilford how much she had always wanted to see the waxworks. And you know when Lady Pembroke mentioned them last week, Georgia said that it was a *vulgar,* disgusting display."

"It is vulgar, but confess, are you not curious to see the Countess of Heningbergh? It's said she gave birth to three-hundred and sixty-five children all at one time and they are all on display."

"It sounds perfectly horrid," Juliana said. "I have no wish to see such a woman."

"No, nor do I, but I *would* like to see the man who fathered them," Johnny said, and grinned as she rapped his arm with her fan.

They paused to wait for Ruth and George Somerset, who were meandering slowly along behind them. Ruth had not wanted to walk in the gardens, but George had persuaded her the walk would be a leisurely one and she could lean on his arm. Juliana studied her friend as they approached, afraid Ruth might be overly tired. One glance at the colour in Ruth's cheeks and the glow in her eyes reassured Juliana. She looked radiant.

They retraced their steps back to the rotunda as the time for the tournament drew close. Lord John had secured them excellent seats in a booth with a good view of the shooting range, and Lady Spalding was overseeing the tea being served when they arrived.

She was too engrossed in the arrangements to notice Ruth slipping a delicate lawn handkerchief from her reticule. Her niece handed it shyly to George Somerset, who placed it reverently inside his coat.

Juliana saw him and smiled. Somerset was tall, taller even than Johnny, and one did not somehow think of such a rough, rugged giant as a romantic. But he was, and in Ruth he had found a girl who stirred his chivalrous instincts. He would be wearing his lady's colours in the tournament just like a medieval knight.

"It is customary to carry a talisman into the competition," Johnny whispered in her ear, startling her. "I will settle for a kiss, Fair Charmer."

"You are incorrigible, sir," she said, laughing up at him. But she undid a blue silk ribbon from her hair and handed it to him. "Good luck, Johnny."

He kissed her hand, and then instead of walking round the stairs, placed one hand on the low railing and neatly vaulted over it. George glanced at Johnny standing cockily outside the booth, and then at the railing. With casual grace, his long legs stepped easily over it. The girls laughed as he clasped Johnny on the shoulder, and waved before setting off down the path.

The tournament was sponsored by the Toxophilite Society, one of London's oldest archery associations, and one which boasted an elite membership. Regular practice and shooting with the long bow were encouraged by many members of the nobility, even the Prince Regent, though no one could recall seeing their portly ruler actually pull one of the long, heavy bows. It required a great deal of physical prowess and athletic ability.

The girls cheered when both Lord John and Somerset hit their marks successfully and moved on to the second round. It was difficult to see the actual targets from the booth, but neither man was eliminated, and they lined up for the final round. George Somerset placed third in the competition and Johnny fourth. His friend chided him when they rejoined the ladies. "If you would only practice a bit more, you could be the best there is."

"Ah, but then what would I have to *aim* for?" Johnny asked, his blue eyes full of lazy good humour.

The girls groaned at the pun, and Lady Spalding told him it would be well if he set his sights higher than where they were at present.

Johnny continued to stare at Juliana. "I could not aim higher than heaven, Lady Spalding," he countered.

"You may have to aim a good deal lower," Juliana said, laughing up at him. "I have never known anyone less angelic."

Lady Spalding declared if they were all going to talk nonsense, they could do it in the barouche and herded her charges through the winding walks and round to the drive where the carriage waited. It appeared everyone who had watched the tournament was leaving at the same time. Gigs, curricles, landaus and phaetons crowded the drive and the lane leading away from the gardens was little better.

Lord John took the reins from his coachman. He intended to manoeuvre the heavy barouche through the crowds himself, and proved the merit of his decision minutes later. Only someone with his skill could have extricated them so quickly from the crush. He had them out of the worst of it and was ready to turn onto Grand Junction Road when George yelled a warning.

It took the ladies unaware. Lady Spalding, sitting in the back next to George, glanced up as he yelled. She saw the bay horses and yellow curricle cutting directly in front of them and closed her eyes in quick prayer. Ruth and Juliana, sitting opposite, saw nothing. They pitched forward as the heavy barouche jerked to an abrupt stop.

Juliana, landing almost in Lady Spalding's lap, was more startled than hurt, and immediately sat up to see what had happened. Johnny had already handed the reins to the coachman and she heard his muttered oath as he jumped down to confront the driver of the curricle. When she saw Claudia Carew, she lifted her skirts and climbed down to hurry after him.

Miss Carew seemed to think it all a good joke. It was she who had been driving Roland Tilbury's carriage, and deliberately cut in front of Lord John. Mr. Tilbury, standing just behind her, looked decidedly embarrassed, but said nothing. Claudia merely laughed when Johnny accused her of driving far too recklessly.

"La, Johnny, you make too much of this. There was no danger and no one was hurt, not even your precious horses."

Juliana saw his eyes darken and his mouth settle in grim lines. She'd never seen Johnny so angry, and when he bit his lip to keep from uttering a retort, she stepped forward. He might be too much of a gentleman to tell this stupid girl what he thought, but nothing would prevent her!

"*I* was thrown from my seat, Miss Carew, and so was Miss Taunton, thanks to your foolishness. We could have been seriously injured."

"Oh, dear me," Claudia said in her high, carrying voice. "I did not know you had the little lame girl with you. I do hope she is all right?"

Juliana knew an urge to slap her and twisted her gloved hands tightly together before replying calmly, "She is, with little thanks to you. But before you drive again, I suggest you get someone to give you lessons, Miss Carew."

Claudia, her face suffused with anger, snapped, "I suppose you think yourself a far better whipster."

"Well, yes rather, if this was any demonstration of your ability."

There were loud chuckles from the gathering crowd and Claudia shrieked, "Why, I could drive rings round you."

Juliana felt Johnny's hand on her elbow as he tried to draw her away, but she shrugged him off. "At least I have never driven into another carriage."

"Ladies," Roland Tilbury pleaded. "I am sure you both handle the reins capably, but—"

"Let us put it to the test," Claudia challenged. "That is, if you dare, Miss Chevron?"

"A race!" Someone shouted from the crowd and the chant was taken up instantly. Juliana looked round in confusion. In her anger, she'd not realized they had attracted so much attention. She saw Lady Spalding frantically waving to her from the carriage and knew she should instantly withdraw. Her behaviour was scandalous.

"Well, Miss Chevron?" Claudia taunted, sensing her advantage. "Do we race or does your bravado only extend to words?"

"Don't be any more foolish than you must, Claudia," Johnny said, turning Juliana away. "Miss Chevron does not—"

"No, I thought as much. She and the little lame girl may be good with words but when it comes—"

"Name the time and place, Miss Carew," Juliana said rashly, swinging round to face her.

"Cornhill, day after tomorrow at three," Claudia said promptly. "We drive from the top of the hill to St.

Michael's, turn in the alley there and drive back. That is, if you *can* drive a curricle?''

''I will see you Wednesday at three, Miss Carew— that is, if you manage to make it home without overturning.''

Johnny's hand on her arm forcibly directed her towards their own carriage and she heard Claudia's contemptuous laugh as they walked away, and raucous, jeering calls from the onlookers. She knew her face was red and kept her eyes steadily fastened on the carriage.

''Chin up, old girl,'' Johnny whispered. ''You're a game one—don't cave in now.'' He felt her hands trembling as he handed her up and smiled tenderly. ''Sure we aren't related, Juliana? That was the bravest, maddest thing I ever saw.''

Lady Spalding took a different view. ''Oh, my dear, whatever will Lady Alynwick say? Quarrelling in public! And with all those people watching. Lord, it will be all over Town before nightfall.''

''It wasn't Juliana's fault, Aunt Ursula. It was that odious Claudia Carew who started it,'' Ruth said, leaning forward and squeezing Juliana's hand. ''I heard what she said, and you mustn't think I mind. I am quite used to it, you know. But, oh, Juliana, it was so wonderful to see the way she looked when you said she needed driving lessons!''

Both Juliana and Lady Spalding couldn't help smiling a little. Only George was quiet and he looked at the other three somberly. ''The thing is, *can* you drive, Miss Chevron?''

LADY SPALDING INSISTED on seeing Juliana home. She took full responsibility for the entire incident and said the least she could do was explain how it had come about to Lady Alynwick. Ruth added her support, and George Somerset adamantly refused to be left out, so it was that the five of them walked into Georgia's private sitting-room interrupting her tête-à-tête with Lord Guilford.

It was difficult to say who was the most surprised. The pair sitting on the low settee rose hastily. Georgia looked becomingly flushed, her blue eyes shining brilliantly. There was an air of confusion about Lord Guilford, and though he tried to disguise it, it was plain he wished them all somewhere far away.

Georgia greeted them sweetly, enquiring if they had enjoyed the tournament and graciously offering tea as they sat down. It was when they all refused any refreshment that she became uncomfortably aware something was very wrong. Ursula Spalding looked too pale and she was working her lips without any sound. Neither Juliana nor Ruth would meet her eyes, and both Johnny and George stood awkwardly silent instead of rambling on in their usual nonsensical fashion.

Lord Guilford rose. "Perhaps it would be better if I left now—"

"No, no," Georgia protested, reaching up to him. "I think I may have need of you. Please stay, Charles." She glanced round and gestured with a jewelled hand. "Will someone please tell me what has happened?"

"Georgia, it was the most unfortunate thing—" Lady Spalding began.

"I take full responsibility. I should have just driven round her and left before—" Johnny started at the same time.

"Juliana was only protecting me," Ruth said in a rush. "You cannot blame her—"

"Oh, Georgia, I am so sorry," Juliana cried. "I never meant to make such a spectacle of myself—"

"One at a time, please. I cannot make any sense of this," Georgia said, holding up a hand. They all fell silent and she focused on her nephew. "Johnny, what has happened? Have you got into another scrape?"

"Not precisely," he hedged. "The thing is, we were leaving the gardens when Claudia Carew cut in front of our carriage. She was driving Tilbury's curricle and came straight at us."

"I will never understand how such a sweet person like Margaret Carew could have such a thoroughly unpleasant daughter," Lady Spalding interrupted, wringing her hands.

"I just barely managed to avoid crashing into her," Johnny continued, "and poor Ruth and Juliana were thrown from their seats."

"Gracious, were you hurt?" Georgia asked, looking at both girls with concern.

"No," Juliana said, answering for them both. She looked directly at Georgia. "I am sorry, and I never meant to cause so much trouble, but she said such odious things—"

"She made several remarks about my being lame," Ruth broke in helpfully.

"And I told her she should have driving lessons, and would be glad to give them to her," Juliana finished.

There was silence for a moment, and Georgia looked at them all in puzzlement. "But I don't see what there is in that to—"

"She challenged Juliana to a race," Johnny said, rushing his fences to get it over with. "Wednesday afternoon down Cornhill."

"Good Lord!" Georgia exclaimed, and reached out unconsciously for Guilford's hand. Her blue eyes beseeched Juliana as she addressed her. "You...you did not agree? Pray, tell me, you did not agree to such a thing?"

Juliana's bowed head and flushed face told all. Georgia turned to Guilford. "What are we to do? Oh, how could that dreadful Carew girl propose such a thing? And on *Wednesday!*"

"Juliana really did not have any choice," Johnny offered. "Claudia goaded her into it, and what with the crowd yelling and all—"

"The crowd?" Georgia murmured, her voice faint with horror. "There were witnesses?"

"A few," he owned. "You know how a crowd gathers when there is an accident..."

Georgia closed her eyes.

Juliana rose swiftly and knelt in front of the older woman, taking her cold hands in her own. "I am truly sorry. I never meant to cause so much trouble."

"Juliana, understand I do not hold you to blame, but you cannot do this. To drive in the Park is one thing, but to actually race in public and on Cornhill of all places—no. You cannot do this. Charles, tell her."

Guilford looked uncomfortable and his hand went instinctively to his cravat. "Truly an unfortunate affair, Georgia, but I don't see how she can draw back now. It's a scandal either way, but if she can carry it off in the right manner—" He broke off, shrugging.

"But on *Wednesday,*" she moaned.

"I don't understand, Aunt," Johnny said. "What difference does it make what day it is?"

"The assembly, you idiotic boy! We just received the vouchers for Almack's this afternoon. But how can

Juliana appear there after the race? The scandal will be on everyone's lips!''

"I think Lord Guilford is right," George said, earning a scathing look from Georgia. "Not my affair, I know, but the thing is to carry it off with a high hand. If we all turn out to watch, what can anyone say?''

"What can anyone say?'' Georgia mimicked. "Oh, you and Johnny are two of a kind. They can say a great deal, and very likely will. You may be sure of that. Claudia will tell her cousin and Percy Cochrane will see to it that the news is all over Town.''

"Lord, I'd forgotten about him," Johnny said, rising and crossing to the sideboard and helping himself to a stiff drink. "But will he spread such a tale? It is not exactly to Claudia's credit.''

"What does that matter? This is her second Season and she has the family name to protect her and is as good as engaged to Tilbury. But Juliana—oh, my dearest. Don't you see? You are not well enough known to live the scandal down. People who do not know you will judge you by this. Why, you may even be snubbed at Almack's!''

"Well, George and I can at least see to that," Johnny said. "Between us and our friends, Juliana will dance every dance but the waltzes. And if you and Lady Spalding support her, we should manage to rub through this tolerably well. The only thing is Percy. Perhaps I should have a word with him.''

"No! I absolutely forbid it," Georgia said, rounding on him. "It would only make matters worse. Promise me you will stay away from him.''

"Your aunt is right, John," Guilford said quietly. "Only let Percy see how disturbed you are, and he will do his worst. Word will spread fast enough as it is.''

"Yes, and what Spencer will have to say about the débâcle, I shudder to think." Georgia sighed.

"Say about what?" a deep voice asked from the doorway.

Seven startled faces turned to stare at the Earl of Granville. Only the ticking of the mantel clock could be heard in the sudden silence.

CHAPTER NINE

JULIANA STARED. The earl, clad in a dark blue riding coat, buff pantaloons and Wellington boots, strolled casually into the room as though his entrance had not discomposed everyone. Nothing in his demeanour indicated that he was aware of the awkwardness of the situation, and he did not utter a word as several people began speaking at once.

Georgia's voice carried above the rest, and she rose to greet him with a show of delight. "Spencer, dear. How wonderful to see you. We were just speaking of you."

"Were you?" he asked dryly, accepting the kiss she bestowed on his cheek and glancing at the others.

"Spence, old boy, you've arrived just in time—" Johnny said, but was cut off abruptly by his aunt.

"Yes, indeed. I was just saying how dreadful it would be if you heard the news before Charles had a chance to speak with you." She gave an unconvincing laugh, and hooked her arm in Guilford's. "You know how gossip spreads in Town, and I fear I've been most indiscreet. Charles was just scolding me. He would have it that we must have your blessing before making our betrothal public."

Guilford, whose cravat seemed to be exceedingly tight, tugged at it uncomfortably.

"How gratifying," Spencer murmured with a lift of his brow. He turned and greeted Lady Spalding politely, spoke kindly to Ruth and then to Juliana. He saw the flush spread up her throat and across the delicate lines of her face.

Lady Spalding spoke into the uncomfortable silence. "Such wonderful news, is it not, Lord Granville? But you will be wishing to discuss it privately, I know. Come along, Ruth, we must take our leave."

"I'll see you home, ma'am," George Somerset quickly volunteered, crossing anxiously to Ruth's side.

"In what?" Johnny demanded. "We came in the barouche, remember? I'll drive them home." He turned to take his leave of Juliana and whispered quietly, "We'll talk about this later tonight. I don't know what she has in mind, but just follow Aunt Georgia's lead."

"You are coming back for dinner, aren't you, Johnny?" Georgia asked, a pleading look in her eyes.

"Wouldn't miss it," Johnny said, and offered his hand to Guilford. He smiled, a mischievous light in his eyes. "Congratulations, sir. I know you and my aunt will deal extremely well together."

Guilford, much to his credit, managed to thank him, accepting the news of his sudden engagement with seeming aplomb. But Johnny saw the way his eyes gazed longingly at the door and thought, were it not for the stranglehold his aunt had on his arm, he would have made good his escape with the rest of them.

Lady Spalding sailed from the room as though she could not wait to leave. The two girls walked out more slowly, Johnny and Somerset strolling behind them. Ruth's auburn head bent close to Juliana's. "I feel as though this were all my fault. Perhaps if I tried to explain to Lord Granville what happened—"

"You are not to blame," Juliana assured her. "It was my wicked tongue which did the damage and I want you to promise me not to worry. Georgia will think of something."

Ruth's dark eyes were filled with remorse, and she impulsively hugged her friend. "Oh, I hope you are right."

Juliana managed a smile as she waved to them from the entrance, but it disappeared as she slowly retraced her steps to the salon. She opened the door and saw Granville sprawled comfortably in a chair opposite the settee where Georgia sat, her hand in Guilford's. The gentlemen rose as she entered, and she hastily bade them be seated, while taking the chair closest to Georgia. Juliana could feel Granville's eyes on her and looked down at her hands.

When he had first arrived, she had known an immeasurable sense of relief and a longing to confess her scandalous behaviour at once. For that one brief moment of madness, she had somehow imagined Granville would set matters to rights. Then Georgia had spoken and Juliana realized the earl would be shocked by her conduct. In her mind, she heard him say that no gentleman would care to marry so notorious a lady as The Fielding. After Wednesday, she would be equally notorious. He would no longer consider her a suitable bride for Johnny.

"Well, Miss Chevron," Granville said, breaking into her thoughts, "it appears there is to be a betrothal in the family. Not quite the announcement I anticipated, but a cause for celebration nonetheless, don't you agree?"

"Why yes, my lord," she answered and managed a tremulous smile for Georgia. "I have not yet had a chance to wish you happy. Have you set a wedding date?"

"Not really." Georgia laughed. "There are so many details to be attended to and you will understand that I am finding it difficult to think clearly just now. And there is the Season ahead of us. When that is over, we shall see. Perhaps in December or January."

Lord Guilford coughed and tugged at his collar. "I owe you an apology, Granville. Should've spoken with you first, I know."

"As my consent is merely a matter of form, there is no harm done." He paused, studying Guilford curiously. "I own I am a trifle surprised, however. Oh, not at the betrothal, but the manner of it. Rather impetuous of you, wasn't it? I would have expected a military man to plan a more orderly campaign."

"I did," Guilford said quietly. He glanced at Georgia, a tender look of pure devotion, before adding, "But even the lowliest soldier knows that when one is given a golden opportunity, one must either seize the moment or lose the battle."

"Really, gentlemen," Georgia protested, waving her fan. "I will not be spoken of as a citadel or some such. Next you will be speaking of storming my walls or laying siege to my ramparts."

"It is the price of wedding a military man, I fear," Granville said with a smile, but he seemed to have lost interest in the conversation and he turned to Juliana. "We civilians owe a great debt of gratitude to the military, do you not agree, Miss Chevron?"

She looked up, her green eyes reflecting her confusion. "Yes, of course."

"And I know you must also agree that Lord Guilford is especially deserving of our thanks."

"Certainly, but I do not see—"

"Let us reward him then with a few minutes alone with his intended. It is only a small measure of our gratitude but one which I am sure will be amply appreciated," he said, rising and extending his hand to her. "I suggest a stroll in the gardens."

She could not help smiling at his elaborate manoeuvring. "And you said your aunt was the strategist in the family!"

Neither Georgia nor Lord Guilford offered Juliana any encouragement to remain. Indeed, her chaperone said the fresh air would do her good and the wide grin on Guilford's face was proof enough of his approval. Juliana reluctantly allowed the earl to place her hand in the crook of his arm and lead her out through the French doors.

She could feel the strength and warmth of his arm through his riding coat and idly wished that circumstances were different. She had been looking forward to his arrival in Town, but now found it difficult to be at ease with him. She could have faced him better if he knew the truth, but Georgia's deliberate deception put her in an embarrassing position.

"You are very quiet, Miss Chevron. Has this military talk put you off or are you thinking of your own possible marriage?"

"Neither, sir," she hedged, and made an effort to speak lightly. "In truth, your aunt has left me little time to think of anything. You would not credit the number of persons with whom I am already acquainted, or the number of small parties I have already attended although I do not make my official bow until Wednesday.''

''Wednesday? Ah, let me guess. My aunt has somehow contrived to secure the coveted vouchers to Almack's.''

She nodded. ''Princess Esterhazy presented them and Johnny is to escort us.''

''I see. I gather our plan is progressing, then? If my brother has agreed to escort you to a function such as that, you may count it a conquest.''

''I count it as a mark of your aunt's influence, though others may not. Johnny's escort has earned me the distinct dislike of one young lady in London.''

He paused and she stood still watching him break off a rose from the large hedge which bordered the walk. His back was to her and she couldn't see his face, but his voice seemed to mock her. ''What, only one?''

''Oh, there are many who envy me, but only one whose dislike is such that it is marked. Are you acquainted with Miss Carew?''

He turned then and presented her with the yellow rose he'd purloined. His hand touched hers and he smiled down at her. ''Are you like a rose then, fallen among the thorns?''

''How can I answer you, sir?'' she said, her dimple appearing. ''If I agree, you will think me conceited in comparing myself to a rose.''

''The simile was mine, Miss Chevron.''

''No, my lord. You did not liken me to a rose, but asked if I was like one. A different thing entirely.''

''Yes . . . yes, it is,'' he murmured, gazing into her green eyes, his hand tightening on hers. He saw her lips open a fraction and fought the urge to lower his head to taste that inviting mouth.

Granville abruptly stepped away from her and Juliana felt as if a cloud had passed over the sun. Glancing down at the rose she held, she saw the drop of blood where a thorn had pierced her finger. She blinked rapidly, trying to concentrate on what he was saying. It was something about Miss Carew.

"Is she a thorn in your side?"

"You may choose to describe her that way," she managed to reply. "Certainly, she would like to inflict whatever pain she could, but I am not her only victim. She behaves horridly to Ruth Taunton."

"Then both you and Miss Taunton should feel flattered," Granville said. They had reached the end of the walk, and with a gentle pressure on Juliana's arm, he turned them back towards the house. "Miss Carew is the sort of female who would not bother with you were you not a threat to her popularity. If she has been behaving horridly, then obviously she must consider you a rival. I suggest you consider her motives and take no notice of her."

Juliana choked back a hysterical laugh. "A pity you were not in Town sooner, my lord. Your advice is . . . is always invaluable."

The earl heard the break in her voice. There was something afoot, and he wished Juliana would confide in him. He patted the slender hand on his arm and spoke quietly, "Is there something more troubling you, my dear? If there is anything I could do, you have only to ask."

She shook her head, unable to speak for the tightness in her throat, and kept her eyes focused on the French doors ahead.

Granville said nothing else. Juliana would not confide in him, but he was convinced his aunt was up to some sort of devilment. Only a fool would have believed that she was discussing her betrothal when he had walked in the door. And Johnny had looked relieved to see him. Johnny had said he had arrived just in time. *For what?*

He held the door open for Juliana to pass through, his mind preoccupied with the puzzle. He barely noticed the maid settling the tea tray and a few minutes later absently accepted the cup his aunt handed him.

"Spencer, dearest, I believe you have arrived just in time to help me with a small problem. My estate manager has written me about some new form of agriculture he wishes to try on the home farm. You know I haven't a head for such details and I thought of you at once. Would you be a lamb and drive down to Alresford and sort it all out? It shouldn't take you more than a few days."

There was an odd light in Granville's eyes as he considered his aunt's request but he nodded agreeably. "Certainly, if you feel I could be of some help, but in light of your engagement, perhaps your intended should be the one to tend to this for you."

Guilford's head jerked up. "Not I! No—I know nothing about agriculture. Egad, Granville. You can't have considered. I'm a military man."

"You *were*," the earl pointed out, smiling. "But now that you've resigned your commission, you'll have to learn to look after my aunt's properties. Alresford is not the only one, you know."

Georgia laid an encouraging hand on Guilford's arm, and spoke to her nephew. "He will, darling, but that sort of thing must be done gradually. Though now that you mention it, this *would* be an excellent opportunity. Charles, why don't you go with Spencer? He

can show you round the estate and it would give the
two of you a chance to discuss everything.''

They both looked at her blankly.

''The marriage settlements, silly.''

Juliana had sat quietly, watching Granville. She had
thought before that there was a flicker of amusement
in his blue eyes, and now she was certain of it. He sat
his cup aside and stood lazily.

''A splendid notion. What do you say, Guilford? We
could drive down on Friday if that's agreeable?''

''No!'' Georgia cried and then hastily recovered. She
smiled up at Granville. ''That is, you must leave at
once. Siddons writes the matter is most urgent.''

A lift of his dark brows was the only sign that the
earl found her behaviour strange. He shrugged elo-
quently and lifted his hands in a gesture of helpless-
ness. ''I would not for the world disoblige you, but I
have business in Town tomorrow and Wednesday. I
could not possibly leave before Friday.''

''What kind of business, Spencer? Surely, it is nothing which could not be put off for a few days?''

''Unfortunately, it is. Tomorrow, I have an ap-
pointment with Lord Spenhaven,'' he said, naming a
gentleman who was almost a recluse as far as the ton
was concerned, but still very active in London's com-
mercial affairs. ''He has arranged time in his schedule
to accommodate me and I could not change the ap-
pointment at this late date.''

''I see,'' Georgia said, barely concealing the relief
she felt. ''Well, then, after your meeting with him. If
you left tomorrow afternoon, you could still be at
Alresford before dusk.''

''It really is unfortunate, but my meeting with him
is not until late afternoon,'' he said, and glanced at

Juliana. "I had hoped to entice Miss Chevron to drive out with me tomorrow morning."

His suggestion caught Juliana unaware. She looked up at him with troubled eyes, torn between a desire to be with him and a need to avoid his company. "I should like that, my lord, but I fear Georgia has plans..."

"No, darling, it's quite all right. I was going to take you with me to call on Lady Pembroke tomorrow but that's of no importance. You run along with Spencer."

"Splendid," he said before Juliana could think of another excuse. "Shall I call for you round noon?"

She nodded and then glanced away. There was something in Granville's eyes which made her uneasy and gave the lie to his casual words. She wished he would leave so she could talk to Georgia.

That lady, however, had very different ideas, and the last thing she wanted was for Spencer to leave the house. She reached up a hand to him. "Do sit down, darling, and have some more tea."

"I really must take my leave, but I shall hope to see you this evening. What are your plans?"

"Why, nothing but a quiet evening at home," Georgia answered, blithely consigning Mrs. Malvern's rout party to the winds. "Johnny shall return soon and I thought we would all have a nice family dinner. You will stay, won't you, Spencer?"

His amusement showed plainly in his eyes and the gentle, mocking smile he bestowed on his aunt. "I really am flattered by this sudden desire for my company, but I must decline. You would not have me sit down in all my dirt, would you? No, do not answer. Even if you were generous enough to overlook my dress, I should be uncomfortable. However, if you will allow it, I shall return for dinner."

Georgia knew she was defeated and did not say another word until the door had closed behind her nephew. She waved her fan vigorously as though the action could somehow help her think. "Well, we must hope that he does not encounter anyone before this evening. It is possible, just possible, I think. Spencer does not frequent any clubs—in his own way he is as much a recluse as Spenhaven—and if we can contrive to keep him here this evening, he may not find out about this dreadful race."

"I think I should just tell him the truth," Juliana said quietly. "He is certain to learn about the race sooner or later."

"Hush, child. Do not even think such a thing. We still have time. I may yet contrive a way to see us through this, but if you confess to Spencer now, we will surely be ruined."

"You . . . you think he would be dreadfully upset?" Juliana asked, a blush stealing up her throat.

"La, my dear. Upset is not the word for it. Spencer is . . . well, he is the earl. It's a proud name he bears, and he would not allow anything to besmirch it. He wants you for the countess now, but if he knew the scandal brewing I fear he would—well, it doesn't bear thinking of. Juliana, darling, you know how fond I have become of you. You must trust me to do what is best for you."

Guilford cleared his throat and when Georgia turned to him, he ducked his head. "None of my business, but seems to me that Johnny is not put off by all this and if *he* wants Miss Chevron, would Granville object?"

Georgia patted his hand. "You really do not understand, Charles, and I will explain it all to you shortly, but believe that I know whereof I speak." She stood up and crossed to Juliana's side, putting an encouraging arm around the girl. "Darling, do try not to worry. Everything will work out for the best. Now, you run along upstairs and rest a bit before dinner."

She gave Juliana no chance to object. Telling Guilford she would return in a few minutes, Georgia walked with her up the broad stairs and handed her over to Milly's care. "See that Miss Chevron rests. No one is to disturb her for any reason."

"Yes, ma'am," the girl said, bobbing a curtsy.

"I shall see you later, darling," Georgia said, lightly kissing Juliana's cold cheek, and then hurrying back to the salon. She closed the door against listening ears and smiled ruefully at Guilford.

"Honestly, Charles, I thought you were going to ruin everything with that nonsense about Johnny."

"I don't see—"

"I know," she said, extending her hands to him. She waited till he crossed the room to her, and then lifted her head for his kiss. "At least something is going right," she whispered a few moments later, resting her head against his shoulder.

"Our timing has always been rotten," he said, dropping a kiss on her brow. "I intend to enjoy the next few hours because I think this dinner tonight is going to be deuced uncomfortable. Now, come sit beside me and tell me what you meant about Johnny."

Georgia laughed lightly, following him to the sofa. She sat down, smoothing her skirts, and leaning back within the circle of his arms. "Johnny doesn't matter one way or another."

"But I thought you said Granville intended Miss Chevron as the future countess. Wasn't that why the pair of you engaged her?"

"It was and I still intend to see her as the Countess of Granville. Only—haven't you noticed how she behaves with Johnny? They are more like brother and sister. She laughs at his advances." Georgia shook her head. "No, I am afraid they do not suit at all."

"Then what are you about, Georgia?"

"She would be perfect for Spencer. The girl worships him, and if you would only open your eyes you could see that he is more than half in love with her. Of course he doesn't know it yet, and I am afraid this scandal may put him off before he realizes what he stands to lose."

GRANVILLE HESITATED outside the town house, and then gave the order to his coachman to drive to King Charles Street, St. James Square. Lady Fitzhugh would not object to his calling in riding dress, and if there was anyone in all of London who knew what was afoot, it would be the redoubtable Maria Croydon, the Viscountess Fitzhugh. She was a law unto herself and never left the elegant town house she'd bought from the Earl of Hardwicke. She had no need to. The wealth and the power she wielded brought London to her.

The earl waited in the vast marble hall while his card was carried into Lady Fitzhugh. Minutes later, her portly butler returned and bowed. Lady Fitzhugh would be pleased to see him, he said, before leading the way to the small salon. Granville had seen the room before but still blinked against the brilliant opulence. The room was decorated in every possible shade of green and pink. Arising from a cloud of rose cushions was an elderly matron of astonishing proportions. Her vast figure was draped in a robe of forest green, and her head was wrapped in a bright, pink turban, secured with a vulgarly large diamond brooch. Lively brown eyes danced in the wrinkled face.

"Granville, dear boy," she purred, extending a pudgy hand for his salute. "I confess I am surprised. I had not expected a call from you quite so soon."

"But you did expect one?" he asked, bowing over the hand and looking up at her in amusement. "Your informants are remarkable, Maria. I have been in Town less than four hours."

She chuckled, a deep throaty sound which shook her vast girth and caused a cascade of ripples across the shimmering green silk robe. "That's what I like about you, Granville. You don't mince words. Not like some of the fools who pass for gentlemen these days." She gestured to a chair while she sank once more into the deep cushions of the sofa. "Shall I ring for refreshments?"

"Thank you, Maria, but no. I can only spare a few minutes. I dropped by on impulse and took a chance on finding you alone."

"You timed it well, my friend. Sally Jersey and that coterie of hers just left. We have perhaps half an hour before anyone else is due. But *quid pro quo*, Granville. Tell me, is that aunt of yours going to bring Guilford up to scratch? I hear he's trailing round after her."

"I believe the matter was just settled this afternoon," the earl said and smiled, remembering the way Charles had looked when Georgia had announced their betrothal. "If all goes well, they shall wed in December."

"December! If I were Georgia I'd see to it at once—given their past history. Nasty bit of business that was marrying her off to Halbert Drayton—no offence intended."

"None taken," he assured her while wondering how to broach his question.

"Out with it, Granville. This isn't the House of Lords, so save your diplomacy for where it will be appreciated. Fair's fair. You told me what I wanted to know—now what is it you want?"

He grinned. "The House would be better off with some of your directness, Maria. If I hesitated, it's only because I am not sure *what* it is I want to know. I suspect Johnny is up to something or involved in some sort of scrape and Aunt Georgia is doing her best to keep it from me." He leaned forward and took her hand in his, his eyes full of serious concern and his lips set in a grave line which deepened the cleft in his chin. "Do you know if Johnny is in trouble? Have you heard anything?"

"Johnny? Why, he has been a pattern card of behaviour since he returned to Town," she said, her brown eyes twinkling. "I thought I could depend on him to liven things up a trifle, but—no, you're on the wrong scent, there."

"But if not Johnny, then why is—Juliana!"

"If you are referring to that beauty your aunt has taken under her wing, you're much closer to the mark," Maria said. She laughed and withdrew her hand as she winked at him. "I hear tell she and Claudia Carew are at each other's throat."

The earl frowned. "She mentioned something about Miss Carew taking her in dislike, but I assumed that was only because of Johnny. Are you saying there is more to this than the usual catwittedness?"

"Depends on how you define catwittedness. In my day a well-bred young lady did not engage in a carriage race down Cornhill, more's the pity. A spunky thing, your Miss Chevron."

"Cornhill! You cannot be serious. Why, that is the steepest hill in London. She could break her neck!"

"I knew I should not tell you. I can see by the look in your eyes you mean to put a stop to it, and it is the most exciting thing to happen in London in years. By this time tomorrow everyone will be talking of it."

"Not if I can help it," he said, starting to rise.

"Sit down, Granville. No sense running off half-cocked. Your Miss Chevron was provoked into it, you know. Claudia Carew is a cunning little baggage who doesn't take kindly to playing second fiddle. One of my boys was there and I had the tale firsthand."

"You are not seriously suggesting that I allow this race?"

"If you force your girl to draw back now, she will never be able to hold her head up in Town. Claudia will see to that. Do you want the child to be shunned?"

"I would rather see her snubbed than with a broken neck!" The earl stood up, hands clenched, and paced the room.

Maria watched him for a moment, her shrewd eyes calculating. "What's this girl to you, Granville?"

"To me? Oh, I...I had hoped she and Johnny would make a match of it. It's time he married and I thought...I hoped the responsibilities of marriage would settle him down."

His back was to her and he didn't see the wide grin which creased her face for an instant. Maria held her amusement, and when she spoke, her voice was solemn. "I see. Of course he could not be expected to wed a young lady involved in such a scandal."

"The scandal be damned! It's Juliana I'm worried about."

"Then sit down and let us see what might be contrived."

CHAPTER TEN

LORD GRANVILLE WAS NOT a vindictive man. His decision not to tell his relations of Lady Fitzhugh's plan was not a conscious desire to exact some measure of revenge. He merely wished to see what lengths his aunt and brother would go to in order to keep the race a secret. And Juliana. His mouth twisted into a grim smile as he thought of the slender, dark-haired girl who had managed to turn his well-ordered life upside down. The foolish little girl who thought she could risk her life without his knowledge or interference. Miss Chevron was in for a surprise.

The smile stayed on his lips as he drove home, remained in place while he changed to evening dress and lingered when he called on Percy Cochrane. He presented his card to the butler, a slender, nervous fellow, who saw the smile and instinctively tried to deny his master to callers.

Percy, on hearing the door knocker and thinking the caller was a crony of his, appeared at the head of the stairs. Seeing Granville he stepped back into the shadows of the hall, but it was too late.

"Shall I come up, Percy, or will you come down?" the earl called. The words were phrased as a question but an order was implicit in the tone.

Percy Cochrane was a cowardly fellow, and had he the least choice he would have avoided Granville like the plague. There was nowhere to hide, however, and with the cunning of a cornered rat, he stepped boldly out. He gripped the railing of the stairs with one hand, and with the other withdrew a delicate lacy handkerchief to dab at his lips. It was heavily scented and the aroma wafted down the stairs before him.

"My dear Granville, this is an unprecedented pleasure. I do not believe you have ever called here before," he said, giving an unconvincing cough which might have passed as laughter. "I suppose I should feel honoured."

The earl watched him descend the stairs and was hard put to conceal his distaste. Cochrane wore a claret cutaway coat, with obviously padded shoulders, over a flamboyant red patterned double-breasted waistcoat that only served to heighten his own natural paleness. His shirt collar was of an absurd height and barely folded over a heavily starched cravat tied in the style of the *Orientale,* forcing his head up and preventing his turning his neck in any direction. His trousers were of the new cossack style, wide cut and fitted at the waist and ankles, which had the advantage of concealing his skinny, unmuscular legs. His feet were encased in black patent-leather shoes with low heels and accented with garish buckles of glittering stones.

Percy felt the contempt in Granville's gaze and deliberately paused on the third step where he could look down at the earl. "Well, sir? To what do I owe this visit?"

"Why, I've come to apologize, Percy. I heard about my brother's . . . prank in holding up your carriage last month. A most unfortunate occurrence, and one which I am sure John regrets."

Percy's eyes narrowed into tiny slits above his beak-like nose, and the whining timbre of his voice rose a notch. "He was fortunate that I was asleep at the time. Had I been awake—" He broke off abruptly at the look in Granville's eyes. A sudden vision of the earl leaping up the steps and those large capable hands at his throat caused a film of sweat to appear on his upper lip. Percy touched his handkerchief to his lips again, and hastily changed tactics. "I trust you will endeavour to teach your brother the rudiments of civilized behaviour, Granville, and we may put the incident behind us."

"Yes, that would certainly be best. So embarrassing were word of the mishap to circulate amongst the ton. Tell me, Percy, just between you and me—is it true you were on your knees begging John for mercy?"

The butler standing discreetly near the hall door smothered a laugh with a fit of coughing.

Cochrane, helpless fury in his eyes, turned on him, snapping, "What are you doing loitering there? I am not paying you to stand about listening to your betters!"

Granville saw the man, his face expressionless, nod and retire behind the hall door, not quite shutting it. He smiled. "Very wise. Servants do talk so, do they not? Amazing how quickly gossip spreads in Town, especially unsavoury tales..."

"All right, Granville. What is it you want? I have better things to do than stand here listening to you cast slurs upon my name."

"Ah, yes, and such a fine name it is, which brings me to my point. I felt sure you would want to lend your honourable name to a certain charitable event which will take place Wednesday afternoon. Lady Fitzhugh is sponsoring it and the proceeds will go to help the orphans.''

"What event? I've heard nothing about a charity ball—"

"You're slipping, Percy. Why, everyone is talking about it, but you mistake the matter. It is not a ball, but an exhibition of horsemanship. Some members of the Four-in-Hand Club are going to demonstrate their skill with the ribbons, and my brother and Lord Somerset will perform some rather daring feats on horseback.''

Percy sniffed, relaxing perceptibly. "What has that to do with me?''

"Why, only that I was positive you would wish to participate, especially as you are always boasting of your skill with a curricle. I assured Lady Fitzhugh that the pair of us would race down Cornhill—for the benefit of the orphans, of course.''

Percy's hand tightened on the railing. He knew what the earl was about now. He'd told Claudia no good would come of her challenge to Miss Chevron.

"You do agree, don't you, Percy, that we should all do our part to help those less fortunate? The proceeds will go to the Foundling Hospital.''

"And if I do not choose to participate?''

The earl withdrew an enamelled snuffbox, and with a deft flick of his wrist, opened the pretty lid. He was elaborately casual as he took a pinch and then allowed his gaze to travel slowly over Percy. "I had hoped your understanding would be such that it would preclude explicit threats, Percy. However, suffice it to say that you *shall* race against me. You *shall* carry your cousin Miss Carew as a passenger. I will carry Miss Chevron as mine. The race will certainly put an end to any such unfortunate gossip which might begin to circulate as to your. . . lack of courage. Is that quite clear?''

''I never thought I would see you resorting to blackmail, my lord,'' Percy said, his tiny eyes narrowing to slits of calculation. ''What do you care about Juliana Chevron?''

The earl restored the snuffbox to his pocket and before Percy realized his intention, had taken the few steps necessary to bring him on a level with the smaller man. Granville looked down at him, anger turning his eyes a pale hard blue, and his voice harsh. ''Let there be no mistake about this. I never wish to hear her name on your lips again.''

Percy cowered back against the railing and gasped as Granville's hand reached out to caress his cravat.

''Do I make myself clear, Percy?''

''Yes, for God's sake, yes,'' he cried, and took a deep breath as Granville released him and stepped back down to the hall. ''I was only speculating—''

''I would not advise your doing so again,'' the earl replied, adjusting the ruffles at his wrist. ''We are agreed, are we not? We race on Wednesday at three? It is a splendid opportunity for you. Who knows? You may even contrive to win.''

''I will be there, Granville. I only hope word of your coercion does not get about.''

''I trust it won't, Percy. It would be most unfortunate for you if it did,'' Granville promised, and turned his back on the hatred spewing forth from Percy's eyes. ''Do not trouble to see me out.''

With Cochrane taken care of, the earl returned to his carriage. The rest of the arrangements he could leave in Maria's capable hands. She would petition the members of the Four-in-Hand Club for their help, and arrange for the seating to be set up, and lackeys to sell tickets. Maria fully intended to make a great deal of money for the hospital. In all likelihood, Juliana's scandalous race would turn into the charity event of the Season. All that was left for him to do was speak to Johnny later this evening. As for his aunt and Juliana... He smiled. Tomorrow would be time enough to tell them. Tonight, he intended to enjoy their manoeuvring. He turned his horses towards Grosvenor Square, wondering what new excuse his aunt would find to send him out of Town.

THE DINNER PARTY that evening was not one of Lady Alynwick's more notable efforts, although Granville enjoyed it immensely. Johnny, too, managed to maintain his usual irrepressible spirits, but to the rest of the guests, dinner was more of an ordeal than a betrothal celebration.

Lord Guilford, the guest of honour, bore the air of a gentleman about to face the firing squad. He made such frequent recourse to his wineglass that his eyes took on a rather glazed look halfway through the dinner, and he replied in monosyllables to the few remarks addressed to him.

George Somerset, who normally could be depended on to follow Johnny's lead, was too intent on putting Ruth Taunton at ease to give either his friend or Lady Alynwick much support. Every time Granville directed a remark to Miss Taunton, George interrupted. His behaviour bordered on rudeness, but earned him a sweet smile of gratitude from the girl beside him.

Ruth, knowing she must keep the race a secret from the earl, suffered an agony of embarrassment every time Granville glanced at her. She was incapable of duplicity. Her guilty blushes and downcast eyes would have alerted the most dimwitted of men that something was afoot.

Her behaviour afforded the earl a great deal of amusement. He smiled at her kindly, resisting the temptation to tease her further, and looked down the table at Juliana. It was she who intrigued him, and he watched her speaking with Lord Guilford. One had to admire the girl's poise, he thought, and wondered what she was planning. Juliana had landed herself properly in the briars and could not possibly sit there looking so beautifully serene if she did not have some sort of scheme in mind. He would have to put a stop to it, whatever it was. He saw the look she exchanged with Johnny. Like two children up to mischief, he thought, and suddenly felt a pang of regret. If he were only younger—

"Will you be returning to Crowley soon, Granville?" Lady Spalding asked, interrupting his thoughts. Georgia had ordered her to keep the earl occupied during dinner, and all her protests had been in vain. She found conversation with Granville difficult at the best of times. He had an acerbic wit, and she frequently felt that she did not understand above half of what he said. Tonight was proving worse than usual, and she would have given it up except for the way Georgia kept frowning at her.

"It will depend on the next few days," Granville replied.

His words sounded ominous to her ears, and the small smile playing about his lips completely unnerved her. She dropped her fork and it fell clattering to her dish. The sound drew everyone's attention.

The earl spoke into the silence as though nothing had occurred. "The weather promises to be fine for the next day or so. Perhaps we should plan an outing for Wednesday. What do you say, ladies?"

It was Guilford who spoke up. "Not Wednesday, Granville. You are forgetting Almack's."

Georgia smiled at her intended, managing to convey with her eyes the gratitude she felt, and lifted her wineglass in a silent toast.

The earl, noting the warm look which passed between them, leaned close to Georgia, asking softly, "Are you quite certain you wish to share this evening? I could take all your guests to the theatre or the opera if you like."

Georgia met his eyes and knew a moment's doubt. She had questioned him extensively when he'd returned and was positive he'd not heard about the race, but there was something, she thought, something which was causing him to behave erratically. Whatever it was, she did not like it. She summoned a smile and managed to thank him sweetly. "That is most thoughtful of you Spencer but you and Johnny are all the family I have. I want my boys near me this evening."

"Yes, I was certain you would say that," Granville replied, and motioned the footman to refill his glass, biding his time. He glanced at Juliana, sitting across from him and next to Johnny. They made a handsome pair, but he wondered if he had not made a mistake in matching her with Johnny. He was beginning to doubt that his brother was capable of controlling her. She was every bit as headstrong as he, and twice as innocent. An old biblical quote came to mind unbidden and he chuckled aloud. "If the blind lead the blind, both shall fall into the ditch."

Georgia rose hastily, signalling to the ladies that it was time to withdraw. She didn't like the look on Spencer's face. "I hope you will not linger long over your brandy, gentlemen. Juliana has promised to sing for us this evening, and Ruth will accompany her on the spinet. I know you will all enjoy their performance."

"I have no doubt of it," Granville murmured, as he politely stood. "I have already been vastly entertained this evening."

"He knows," Juliana whispered to Georgia as they left the room.

"Impossible, child. He has not seen a soul who could—"

"He does," she insisted. "He was toying with us during dinner. We should have told him the truth this afternoon."

"Nonsense. You are making too much of a few remarks. I will grant you that he realizes we are keeping something from him, but he cannot possibly know what. If he had—well, he would have stormed in here this evening demanding an accounting."

Her remark gave Juliana pause. It was true. She could not imagine Granville's calmly accepting the idea that she was to race Miss Claudia Carew down a public thoroughfare in front of half of London. She knew from Johnny of the tremendous scolds Granville had given him on occasion. Hung him out to dry, Johnny had said. Perhaps Georgia was right, but that did not alter the fact that her own behaviour was reprehensible. She owed it to Granville to tell him the truth—even if it meant an end to her position and a return to the drudgery she had known before.

The thought saddened her. She did not mind the hard work and plain clothes, although that would be difficult enough to face after the past six weeks, but she could endure that. It was the earl's disapproval which she dreaded—and the idea of never seeing him again. Or Johnny. Or Georgia. Her throat contracted, and it was not easy to force out the gay lilting words of the ballad Ruth was playing with trembling fingers.

Juliana's low, sweet voice floated across the room, imbuing the melody with a haunting, aching wistfulness which the composer never intended.

SHE WAS READY when the earl called for her at one the next afternoon and had taken particular pains with her attire. The dark green walking dress, and its matching pelisse trimmed with black ribbons, suited her admirably. Her small green bonnet curved prettily over her brow, and the ostrich plume dyed green lay softly against her dark curls. Although her complexion was a trifle wan and the darkness beneath her eyes attested to a sleepless night, she thought she looked well over all. She hoped so. She planned to tell Granville the truth this afternoon, and it might be the last time she would ever see him. She wanted him to remember her dressed in all her finery and not as the little brown wren who had answered his advertisement.

Granville was in excellent spirits and greeted her cheerfully, his eyes full of warm approval as he admired her attire. "That colour suits you well, Miss Chevron," he said, and thought instantly of a certain pear-shaped emerald pendant which had belonged to his mother. The deep green of the jewel would draw out the colour of Juliana's eyes. He could picture in his mind how well it would suit her, the delicate gold chain against her neck and the emerald falling enticingly between her breasts.

Juliana withdrew her hand from his tightened clasp, wondering why was he staring at her so oddly. "Thank you, my lord," she murmured, preceding him through the door.

The earl nodded to Grim, making an effort to banish such unworthy thoughts of Juliana from his mind. He feared he was turning into one of those repellent old men who ogled young beauties and amused themselves with lascivious thoughts. Perhaps, he mused, it was time he paid another visit to Annie Margate. He was surprised to realize it had been over two months since he'd thought of the young opera dancer. He had enjoyed a dalliance with the girl for several years, and it was his custom to pay her a call as soon as he arrived in Town. The idea did not hold its usual appeal, however, and he had to once again check his thoughts as he watched Juliana's slender figure swaying before him.

She paused, surprised to see the curricle drawn up before the house. She had assumed Granville would use his Town carriage.

"I have one or two calls to make and then I thought you might like to take the reins," he explained, seeing her surprise. "Driving is like any other skill. You must practice or you will lose your touch."

"How thoughtful of you," she said, allowing him to help her up. Driving a curricle was the last thing in the world she wished to think about, but even so she could not help but admire the skill with which he handled the showy roan horses. It was some minutes before she became aware that they had entered a squalid section of London. Many of the houses had boarded-up windows and the streets were heavily littered. She glanced around in confusion. "Where are we going, sir? I do not recognize this part of Town."

"A bit of business I must attend to. Have you heard of the Foundling Hospital?"

"Only vaguely. I believe it is where unwed mothers take their children for adoption, is it not?"

"If they are fortunate," he replied, glancing down at her. "The hospital is much in demand and regrettably cannot accept all the children brought to the gates. You would not credit the number of unwanted children in London."

They were driving through a disreputable area, and she shivered at the sight of several urchins in the alleys. They were all poorly clothed and sadly undernourished.

"The hospital accepts infants under twelve months if the father has deserted the mother," Granville was explaining. "Then the children are sent into the country with foster parents until they are four or five years old. We bring them back to the hospital then to educate them. The boys are indentured at fourteen, and we keep an eye on them until they finish their apprenticeship. A great many of them join the army. The girls are trained as ladies' maids. My aunt's girl, Milly, comes from the hospital, and so did Dorcas, the maid who looked after you at Crowley."

"And the children who are not accepted? What happens to them?"

Granville lifted a hand from the reins and gestured at the streets. "They manage as best they can. Many do not live above eight or nine years. What we need is more homes. The Foundling Hospital can only accept about a third of all those who apply."

It was a depressing picture he painted and one she vowed to remember if ever she began feeling sorry for herself. At least she had been raised in a real home with a mother who had loved her. The sight of the orphans in the streets haunted her. "How do they determine which children to accept?" she asked. It was not a decision she would want to have to make.

"The luck of the draw. The mothers gather at the gate and are given a chance to draw a coloured ball from a bag. If she draws a white ball, the child is admitted tentatively, and must still pass a medical examination. A red ball means the child will be put on a waiting list and if one of the children admitted is found to be suffering from an infectious disease, then that child will be admitted in its place. If the poor mother draws a black ball, then both she and the child are asked to leave. It is not the best of systems—only the best we can do at present. We are constantly in need of funds, which is something I want to discuss with you later. I am helping to sponsor an exhibition, and the proceeds will go to the Foundling Hospital."

"I should be pleased to help, of course," Juliana assured him, glancing up at his profile. Granville was smiling, though there was nothing amusing about their conversation. She had no time to question him, however, as he brought his team to a halt before the gates. The young man inside recognized Granville and swung the gates open to admit his carriage. Juliana looked back at several young women, babes in arms, waiting forlornly outside.

A few minutes later they were inside a large, gracious room. The Court of Governors room, Granville explained, and asked her to wait there for a few moments while he conferred with one of the matrons.

Left alone, Juliana explored the room. A plate beneath one of the sizeable wall paintings identified it as the work of William Hogarth. She recognized other paintings by Reynolds and Gainsborough and admired the seascapes by several lesser known artists.

"There is an exhibition here every three or four months," Granville said, coming up quietly behind her. "Most of the artists donate all their proceeds to the hospital."

"You are certainly well informed, my lord."

"I should be. My grandmother was one of the original twenty-one ladies who petitioned the King for the hospital. My mother served on the Board of Governors and now I sit in her place. Sort of a hereditary obligation."

"A worthy one, and I should be honoured if I could help in some small way," she said.

"Oh, never doubt it, Miss Chevron. You shall be of inestimable help, and I believe we will raise a great deal of money for the foundlings. Now, there is one more call I must see to before your driving lesson."

He escorted her out and did not see her drawn, worried frown. The time was near when she would have to confess her folly and watch the warm regard in his eyes change to chilly disapproval. Juliana remained quiet, her thoughts disturbing as the earl drove them skilfully through London. She did not stir until he brought his team to a halt.

"To your right, Miss Chevron, is the Royal Exchange," Granville said, pointing to a massive portico fronted by eight Corinthian columns. "At the bottom of the hill lies St. Paul's Cathedral. You can see the dome there in the distance.''

Juliana looked down the steep hill. There seemed to be a number of merchants lining the streets, and she saw the signs of several noted booksellers. Traffic was brisk and pedestrians weaved in and out among the carriages, creating a tumult of confusion.

The earl waited his opportunity and moved their curricle in among the traffic. He kept tight control over his horses, narrowly missing a young boy who darted across the street and the mongrel pup which blindly followed the boy.

Juliana held tightly against the seat of the curricle. The grade was so steep that she feared she would pitch forward, and it was not until they turned onto Lombard Street that she breathed easily again. She glanced at Granville, wondering if he had a particular motive in driving her through this part of Town. He sat relaxed against the squabs, whistling a quiet tune and looking as though he had not a care in the world.

''I apologize for driving through this part of London, Miss Chevron, but I had a particular wish to see that street. It is where the exhibition for the Foundling Hospital will take place.''

''Oh, I see.''

''Not yet, but you will,'' he answered. ''That street we just drove down is called Cornhill. I believe you are familiar with the name.''

Juliana turned white, the blood draining from her face.

Granville manoeuvred his team to a neat stop just inside the entrance of a small park. He signalled to his tiger, and the boy jumped down and ran round to hold the horses' heads. The earl stepped down and reached up a hand to Juliana. "Come, my dear, let us stroll a little."

She gave him her hand and stepped down without conscious thought. Her palms beneath her gloves were damp and she felt nauseated. As soon as her slippers touched the ground, she closed her eyes for a moment, hoping her dizziness would pass.

Granville waited patiently, and then placed her hand in the crook of his arm, drawing her along a dirt path. He was silent for several moments, and when he spoke a hint of sorrow coloured his voice. "I had hoped you would confide in me, my dear."

"I intended to," she said softly, her head bowed. "I knew it was useless to try to keep it from you."

"Why did you?" he asked, curious.

"We...that is, I knew you would be angry, that you would disapprove. Georgia said you would never forgive me."

"Which only goes to prove that my aunt is not quite the infallible authority on gentlemen she believes."

The teasing note in his voice made her look up. She saw the tenderness in his eyes and the sympathetic smile on his lips, and a surge of hope filled her. "You are not angry?"

Granville fought an urge to caress her cheek and gestured to a nearby bench. "Let us sit down for a minute. Of course I was angry that you would risk your neck in such a stunt—but I heard the entire story and I will own that the provocation was great."

She smiled, a hesitant, tremulous effort and was hardly aware that her hand rested in his. "But the scandal—Georgia said you would be furious and—"

"And what did you think? Do I seem such an old curmudgeon to you that I would condemn you out of hand?"

"No, my lord," she said, suddenly shy of him.

"Then could you not trust me?" he asked. There was no shade of reproach in his voice, only the faintest trace of disappointment. "Well, never mind. Let me tell you what I have arranged."

He outlined the plans for the sporting exhibition, and Juliana listened with glowing eyes and growing excitement, her hands holding on to his tightly. "I do not know how to thank you, sir," she said, looking up at him. "May I?" she asked, and without waiting quickly kissed his cheek.

It was the lightest of caresses, just a feathery touch of her lips, but it burned his skin and only her hands holding his kept him from pulling her close and kissing her properly.

She sat back, her eyes sparkling. "This is wonderful. Does Johnny know?" She stood up, unable to remain still and danced away a step. "I cannot believe it. I was so dreading tomorrow, and now it will all be perfectly splendid."

He watched her while somehow managing to keep a smile on his lips. For that brief, mad instant when she had kissed him, he had thought there might be a chance. Then she had asked about Johnny. It was only natural, he supposed, that she should care for his brother. Johnny was younger, handsome and charming and had half the girls in London at his feet while he was older, greyer and too stiff rumped to appeal to a girl like Juliana. Which was probably why she had not confided in him. She was sure he would have disapproved. And the kiss—it was the kiss a young girl would bestow fondly on a favoured older brother or uncle.

Juliana danced back again, extending her hands. "May we walk? I cannot bear to be still now. How can you just sit there?"

CHAPTER ELEVEN

GRANVILLE, HAVING HAD the forethought to lease a room on the upper floor of a coffee-house situated in the middle of Cornhill, seated his party solicitously. Juliana, Ruth, Lady Spalding and Georgia sat in the four chairs before the window. Lord Guilford stood protectively behind the ladies and would remain with them during the exhibition. Granville, glancing at his watch, estimated they had at least an hour before the Four-in-Hand Club would arrive. Then he and Juliana would make their way to his waiting curricle.

Juliana, watching the people streaming through the street beneath them, could not believe that London was thin of company. Georgia had said a great many people had not yet returned to Town, the Season having just begun, but the horde of people gathering for the race was the largest crowd Juliana had ever seen. She peered ahead, straining her eyes for a glimpse of Johnny or George Somerset. They had left the room moments earlier to take their place in what promised to be a sort of equestrian parade.

Ruth saw the gentlemen first and waved, pointing them out to Juliana. Her eyes were sparkling, and the excitement had flushed her cheeks a becoming colour. "Doesn't George look splendid?" she whispered, her gaze steady on his tall, slender build.

Juliana nodded, but her attention was distracted by a group of oddly dressed gentlemen. They wore dark blue frock coats with large brass buttons, blue-and-yellow-striped waistcoats with white corduroy breeches to the knee and conical hats with wide brims. One or two of the group had on large drab driving coats which reached down to their ankles, and were adorned with huge mother-of-pearl buttons. Juliana could not help staring. The coats had above a dozen capes and the gentlemen had stuffed large bouquets of bright yellow flowers in the buttonholes.

Ruth laughed at her astonishment. "That's Sir John Lade in front and Tom Akers beside him. They belong to the Four-in-Hand Club and, my dear, if you think their dress odd, never say so. It is considered a mark of distinction and privilege."

Juliana shook her head at the folly of such gentlemen and glanced back at Granville. He was dressed conservatively as usual in a knee-length black frock coat, buff pantaloons and black Hessian boots. She thought his understated style far more elegant than the flamboyant dress of the Four-in-Hand Club.

Granville saw her glance and smiled down at her. "Lady Fitzhugh has done amazingly, has she not?"

"It is extraordinary," she said and gestured to the carnival-like atmosphere in the street below. "I cannot believe she was able to arrange everything in so short a time. I only wish she were here that I might thank her."

Georgia, seated next to her, patted her hand. "Lady Fitzhugh will be the one expressing her gratitude, child. This exhibition will raise a great deal of money for the Foundling Hospital, and that is all because of you. And let me tell you, it is no little thing to have a person like Lady Fitzhugh in your debt."

Juliana smiled ruefully. To hear Georgia speak, one would think the race had been contrived from the beginning solely for the benefit of the orphans. She had not been the least surprised when Granville had told her the night before about the exhibition. He had wanted to keep Georgia in the dark until this morning, but Juliana had pleaded with him to tell his aunt of their plans and the earl had yielded gracefully.

Georgia had not shown the least remorse for deceiving her nephew, but had hugged Juliana warmly. "You see? I told you we had nothing to fear and that everything would turn out perfectly splendid."

Granville had merely laughed at his aunt, but Juliana had been indignant that so little credit was given to the earl. In her eyes, he had behaved magnificently and she'd said so to Georgia after he'd gone.

"But of course, darling. I never doubted he would," Georgia had replied, her blue eyes wide with astonishment that anyone would presume to think otherwise.

"Then *why* did we not tell him the truth at once?"

"A matter of timing, darling. Had we told Spencer sooner, the results might have been vastly different," she had replied airily. Her eyes had twinkled mischievously as she'd added, "And you must own that it was an opportune time to bring Charles up to the mark."

"Georgia! Did you deliberately—"

"Hush, child. You will learn that gentlemen must be led, for their own good, of course. Why, if I had been foolish enough to leave matters in Charles's hands, it might have been another year before he proposed and we have lost enough time. Now, do not look like that, Juliana. I promise you, he will be the happiest of men. I intend to take very good care of Charles, and once he has recovered from his initial surprise, he will be well pleased.''

Juliana glanced round, remembering the conversation. She saw Lord Guilford hand Georgia a cup of hot tea and the look of devotion on his face was a testimonial to the truth of Georgia's words. His eyes had lost the pinched look of the past few days, and he did, indeed, look well pleased with his situation.

''I think they are ready to start,'' Ruth said, drawing Juliana's attention back to the street. It had been cleared of all the pedestrians, though crowds three and four persons deep lined the sides. She could see the people craning their necks as they looked up the hill.

The noise dwindled and the sound of a bugle could be heard, signalling the approach of the first carriage. It was a yellow-bodied phaeton drawn by four superbly matched bay horses, their silver harnesses glinting in the sunlight. The driver wore the garb of the Four-in-Hand Club and shouts of ''Sir Frederick'' could be heard from the street as the carriage passed. A pretty young girl, wearing a yellow and black pelisse and a large, heavily flowered bonnet, sat beside him, waving gaily at the crowd. Two footmen in rich green-and-gold livery rode on the back, their silver bugles raised.

''Sir Frederick Agar,'' Georgia said, quizzing glass to her eye. ''And I believe that is Miss Ramsey beside him.''

They could see the carriages lining up behind him, and Juliana was astonished at their number. They were all yellow-bodied carriages, some phaetons, some custom-built coaches and all drawn by four beautifully matched horses. Bays appeared to be the favourite colour, but there were a few teams of chestnuts and one gentleman drove four very dark black horses which set the crowd to cheering.

Juliana felt a hand on her shoulder.

"It is time we left," Granville said quietly and drew back the chair for her.

She felt a knot tightening in her stomach, but managed a nervous smile as she rose. Ruth pressed her hand sympathetically and Georgia stood to give her a light kiss.

"Remember, darling, carry it off with a high hand and you will do us all proud."

Juliana, sitting on the high seat of the curricle next to Granville, unconsciously straightened her back and lifted her head. The turmoil inside her made her oblivious to the admiring stares of the crowd, and she had not the least notion that she looked like a Queen sitting proudly beside her consort.

Claudia Carew, sitting beside Percy in the curricle drawn up opposite them, saw only Juliana's outward poise and snapped at her cousin, "You had better win this race or we shall be the laughing-stock of Town. I was a fool to ever let you talk me into this."

Percy's thin lips set in a sulky line. In truth, Claudia had laughed at his suggestion that she ride with him and had insisted on the original race against Miss Chevron. Only his threat of revealing several of her past indiscretions had persuaded his cousin to relent. Her lack of faith in his driving skill had nettled him, and he was determined to show her and everyone else that he was a better man than Granville.

He tightened the reins and glanced scathingly at the greys the earl was driving. They did not look like anything out of the common to him, and in fact appeared a trifle sluggish. His own chestnuts were showy animals and full of juice, already straining on the ribbons. He felt a rush of confidence and his thin chest puffed out a little. He would win this race one way or another, and if Granville proved troublesome, well, he still had an ace to play.

The earl adjusted his reins and nodded to his groom to stand away. The race was of little importance to him and he was of half a mind to allow Percy to win. A victory might do much to lessen the man's vituperative tongue, whereas a loss would only inflame Cochrane to work whatever mischief he could.

The starter stepped out, lifting his pistol. Granville felt Juliana tensing beside him. "Don't look down," he advised softly. "The road may be steep, but I promise you I shall not overturn us. You will enjoy the race more if you sit back and just watch the crowd."

She smiled her thanks, knowing he had sensed her fear and then looked towards the crowds lining the street. She was listening to the shouts of encouragement and watching the grinning faces when the pistol went off and the curricle shot forward. Juliana braced herself against the seat and steadfastly watched the crowds of people flash past. She caught a glimpse of a redheaded boy and realized belatedly that it was Willie with Anna and her husband just behind him, all wildly cheering.

Percy's carriage nosed ahead of them and then widened their lead by a length. She saw Claudia glance back, a gloating smile on her face, and Juliana looked up at Granville. He seemed unconcerned and continued to hold the greys steady as they plunged down the steep hill.

"Come on, gov', spring 'em!" someone shouted from the crowd. "I've a bundle laid on you!"

The curricle ahead careened wildly and the noise from the crowd swelled to an ear-splitting crescendo. Granville flicked his whip over his horses' heads and his team narrowed the gap to half a length.

Juliana closed her eyes, fearing they would crash into the other carriage, but could not bear not knowing what was happening and seconds later opened her green eyes wide. They were within inches of Percy's carriage, and she saw him glance back over his shoulder. A second later, he pulled his team to the left and Granville checked as the curricle in front of them swayed alarmingly. They were approaching the alley where they were to turn and the earl allowed Percy the lead.

She saw Percy's triumphant sneer as he passed them on the way out of the alley and saw his whip flail mercilessly against the flanks of his chestnuts. A groan went up from the onlookers as Percy started his team up the steep hill.

It took only a moment for Granville to turn his own cattle and then they were racing after Cochrane. The chestnuts seemed to be tiring and the earl slowly lessened the distance between them. Her heart beating erratically, Juliana glanced up towards the sky, offering a silent prayer to the gods. It was the purest chance that she saw the boy on the roof of one of the buildings. Her mouth opened to scream as she saw him raise his arm back and a stone come sailing towards them.

The missile found its mark, hitting the shoulder of the grey horse on Granville's side. The horse reared up even as Juliana shouted a warning and the crowd nearest them scattered riotously, fearing a runaway. The horse was bolting, plunging ahead madly, and she could see the sweat on the grey's neck glistening in the sun.

The earl did not rein the team in as she expected, but eased up on the reins, giving the frightened grey his head. The stallion surged forward wildly, pulling their carriage in his wake. Juliana bit her lips, terrified the horse would verge into the crowd and trample someone, but Granville was somehow managing to hold the team in the street. She glanced at him, the calm lines of his face abating some of her fear. The movement of his strong, capable hands was barely perceptible as he manipulated the reins, allowing the momentum the scare had given his team to carry them easily up the hill.

The greys were under control—of that much she was certain as they drew near Percy's team. She saw Cochrane glance back and, seeing Granville gaining on him, swerve his team to the right, blocking the road. The earl checked slightly and brought the greys as close to the right as the crowds would allow. Percy saw him and steered his chestnuts directly in front of them as they approached the crest of the hill.

Juliana saw only a flash of movement and then they were dashing up on Percy's left and the two curricles were nearly even. The chestnuts were labouring hard, their coats wet with effort. Percy laid into them with his whip but Granville's greys drew inexorably ahead and she heard Cochrane's curse as they flew over the finish line, a full length in front of the chestnuts.

The crowd was cheering wildly, calling Granville's name and closing in around the curricle. He stood, lifting his hat to the crowd, and the roar of their approval was deafening. He held out a hand to Juliana, and she hesitantly rose to stand beside him.

"Smile, my dear, and wave," Granville murmured.

Juliana lifted a gloved hand, smiling at the shining, good-natured faces surrounding them. They had survived the race, but could they survive their enthusiastic well-wishers? The curricle rocked slightly as the crowd pressed against it, and she was thankful for the pressure of the earl's hand in her own. A glance at the horses assured her they would not bolt, not with Granville's groom at their heads, and then she saw Johnny and Somerset making their way through the crowd.

"They're selling ale in the Royal Exchange!" she heard them shouting as they manoeuvred through the throng of people. "Let's drink a toast to the grand old man." The idea was taken up and the men, clapping one another on the shoulders, began to turn away and a small space was cleared round the carriage.

Granville vaulted down and then turned to help Juliana, but Johnny was before him. His strong hands steadied her and she thanked him warmly, more pleased than she would own to have her feet safely on the ground again.

"Well done, old man," Johnny said, turning to Granville and offering his hand.

"Thank you," he said, shaking hands briefly. "But was all that 'grand old man' nonsense truly necessary?"

"Don't hold me accountable for that," Johnny said, his eyes full of laughter. "The crowd was shouting it during the race, but I rather thought it suited you. Granville, the grand old man. You should be flattered."

"It is the epithet of 'old' to which I object," the earl replied softly, but no one heard him. Johnny was enthusiastically recounting the race with Juliana and

Somerset, and the earl took advantage of their distraction to see to his horses.

"Wonderful race, sir," his groom said with a wide grin as he approached.

Granville merely nodded, his eyes riveted on the splotch of red marring the neck of his grey. His mouth set in grim lines as he thought of Percy. The man could have won the race easily but had overplayed his hand. Granville had not intended to seriously challenge him—not until he'd seen the stone striking his horse. He looked round, but neither Percy nor his cousin were anywhere in sight. Their curricle had disappeared.

GEORGIA STOOD NEXT to the earl at Almack's later that evening, watching approvingly as Juliana performed the graceful steps of the quadrille with Johnny. They made a splendid couple, and Georgia thought Juliana particularly in looks. Of course it had helped that the child had been besieged with partners. There was scarcely a gentleman present who had not pressed for an introduction or a dance. The equestrian exhibition had been an unqualified success, and much of the credit had been given, however mistakenly, to Juliana.

Granville watched, but his expression held less than pleasure. He had not wanted to attend the assembly, but Georgia had persuaded him that his presence was necessary and he had reluctantly agreed. The night seemed inordinately long, and he had suffered through endless congratulations on the race when all he wanted was to be left in peace. He thought of the calm and quiet of his library and made up his mind to leave as soon as he could escape his aunt's vigilance.

His eyes narrowed, he watched Juliana laughing up at his brother and was not aware of the slender, exotic beauty who materialized at his side. The lady had to tap him on the arm with her fan to attract his attention, and he glanced down into her amused eyes.

"Countess Lieven," he said, bowing over her hand and granting the lady one of his rare, warm smiles.

"You seem preoccupied this evening, my friend," she said, with an arch look before glancing out at the floor. "I am surprised you have not led Miss Chevron out. Everyone expects it after the race."

"That is what I have been telling him, countess," Georgia said, sensing an ally.

"I am sorry to disappoint then, but Miss Chevron's dances are all spoken for," Granville said.

"Except the next, which is a waltz, and Juliana has not yet received approval to dance it," Georgia pointed out helpfully.

The Russian countess had it within her power, as one of the patronesses, to permit Juliana to perform the waltz. She was not averse to doing so, for she was generally good-natured and only took offence when those of less than noble birth dared to presume on her acquaintance. Miss Chevron was well born and much sought after. One of the other patronesses was certain to grant the girl the privilege of waltzing if the countess did not. She looked from Granville's stony countenance to the dark-haired beauty on the dance floor and nodded.

The earl, seeing her amusement and where it was about to lead, tried to escape, but Georgia held his arm firmly, while the countess smiled up at him.

"Yes, I believe it would be most fitting if you, dear Granville, were to lead Miss Chevron out."

"Thank you, countess," he replied, carefully masking his annoyance. "But I believe my brother has a prior claim."

"No, do not gainsay me, Granville. We must all bow to the dictates of the public and it is you, not the Madcap, the public wishes to see. You and the pretty little Miss Chevron."

There was nothing he could say. The quadrille over, Johnny appeared with Juliana on his arm. Granville did not hear the rest of the countess's words as he noted how well Juliana's white satin gown fitted her slender form. A delicate wreath of tiny, white roses nestled in the dark black curls of her hair, and his eyes followed the enticing trail of one long tress lying against her slender neck. She turned her head then, her green eyes glowing beneath dark lashes, and smiled up at him as she gave him her hand.

He had no choice then and bowed formally before leading her out on the floor to take their position. There was a scattering of applause as the orchestra began, but Granville did not hear it. Placing one hand on her back, he had to restrain an insane urge to pull her closer, to feel her slender body pressed against his, and to breathe in the enchanting scent of roses wafting from her hair. Juliana tilted her head back, laughing softly. It was an exhilarating sound, and his own lips formed a smile at her innocent enjoyment. It was fortunate the child had no way of knowing the lascivious thoughts running through his mind.

"Thank you, my lord," she said softly.

"For what, little one?" The words were a caress and escaped his lips before he could retract them. He turned her then, in a dizzying whirl meant to distract them both.

Her happiness spilled over in a shower of laughter as soft as raindrops. ''Why, for waltzing with me, for rescuing me from scandal, for winning the race, for... for being everything a gentleman should be.''

Granville looked down into her eyes, unable to answer. He spun her around, revelling in the soft feel of her. So this was what it was like to hold moonlight in your arms, he thought, and smiled. Shimmering, magical moonlight, golden and priceless, the stuff dreams were made of. It was madness, pure madness. But everyone should have one such moment of madness. One moment to last a lifetime.

He moved her through the long ballroom, oblivious to the crowds watching and both of them unaware that they were alone on the dance floor. The other couples had slowly withdrawn and stood silently watching. There was a dreamlike quality to the tableau before them. The tall, elegant gentleman in black and the slender beautiful girl in white floated across the room as though they were one.

The music ended with a last flourish, and Granville swept Juliana into a series of rapid turns which had both their heads spinning. The burst of loud applause and buzz of conversation brought them to their senses but could not lessen their joy.

The earl bowed and escorted Juliana back to Georgia's side before excusing himself. He wished there was somewhere in the rooms of Almack's that he could get something stronger than lemonade to drink, and then ruefully thought that it was just as well there was not. Juliana was intoxicating enough by herself. What he needed was a moment alone to regain some measure of control. He politely thanked the many people complimenting him, eluded several talkative dowagers and slipped into a small, empty alcove.

He heard the chatter of several persons passing and thought he recognized Maria Sefton's voice.

"Now that is how the waltz was meant to be performed," the lady was saying. "Why, I vow, it was like watching a play."

"More like a farce," a loud, nasal voice replied. "I thought it was disgraceful. Why, Granville was practically making love to that girl right on the dance floor. It should not be allowed!"

"Oh, do try not to be so ridiculous, Clara."

"I know what I saw, Maria, and if any gentleman ever behaved to my daughter like that, well, you may be sure the banns would be read before he was much older."

"I tell you, you are making too much of this. Why, Granville is too old for that girl and more to the point, she is all but betrothed to his brother. He was just being kind to her."

Granville waited until the voices had passed from his hearing before stepping out of the alcove. The elation he'd felt while dancing with Juliana had vanished, leaving him unbelievably weary, and he made his way towards the steps. Mr. Willis stood at the bottom, and he spoke briefly to the man, directing him to inform his aunt that he would see her on the morrow. Johnny could escort the ladies home. They had no need of him. He stepped out into the cool night air and looked up at the stars. It had been just a moment of madness, nothing more.

JULIANA LOOKED searchingly around the room, but Granville had disappeared. She could not believe he would leave without a word to her and her eyes kept straying to the door, but there was no sign of the earl's tall, distinguished figure. It was Johnny who took her in to supper and who tried to tease her back into good spirits.

"Well, Miss Carew not only lost the race, but has lost her position as the toast of the ton. You, my dear Juliana, are the new reigning belle, and an unqualified success. Can you not at least smile?"

She smiled but it was a poor effort, and he saw the strain round her mouth and the shadows in her eyes.

"I am sorry, Johnny. I seem to have the headache," she said, toying listlessly with the lobster patty on her plate.

"I do have a cure for that, my fair enchantress," he whispered. "Slip out with me and I will take you for a moonlight drive. I know a place where we can see all London spread beneath us and the stars look so close you can reach out and touch them."

She shook her head, not even bothering to rebuke him.

"Like that, is it?" he asked quietly, and touched a finger gently to her cheek.

Juliana blinked back the threat of tears. "I do not know what you mean, Johnny. It is merely that I am tired and . . . and I have the headache."

"And I am not the one who could make it disappear, am I? Well, if I must lose you to someone, then I am glad it's Spence. What are you going to do about it?"

She shook her head helplessly, the warm sympathy of his voice undoing her composure. "There is nothing I can do . . ."

"Oh, is there not? And you a protégée of my aunt's! Does she know, by the way?"

"No." She sniffed and took a sip of water. "No one does, at least I hope not, and it's no use. Granville doesn't . . . he doesn't feel—"

"Now, don't go crying on me. Matters aren't as hopeless as you seem to think. These things have a way of working out. Why, just look at my aunt and Guilford. No one would have bet a groat she'd end up with him, and here she is planning her wedding."

Juliana gave him a watery smile. "Thank you, Johnny, but it is not at all the same. Please, just forget this." She discreetly wiped her tears away and lifted her chin. "I am leaving tomorrow."

He whistled soundlessly. The situation was worse than he had guessed.

CHAPTER TWELVE

JULIANA, AFTER DISMISSING MILLY, walked restlessly around her bedchamber, rehearsing what she would say to Georgia. When telling Johnny of her intention to leave, she had spoken impulsively, but she knew as soon as the words were said that it was the right thing to do. Under the circumstances, she could not possibly remain in the earl's employ. He had engaged her to entice his brother into matrimony and now, of all the gentlemen in London, Johnny was the last man she could wed.

How could she even begin to contemplate marriage with him when she was in love with Granville? Juliana sank into the cushions on the settee and picked up a pretty needlepoint pillow, hugging it to her. Granville. She had suddenly realized how much she had come to care for the tall, handsome earl when they were waltzing together. And for one brief moment, she had thought he cared for her, but of course that was preposterous, mere wishful thinking on her part. He was still devoted to Cynthia's memory, and even if he were not, he could never care for someone like her. Someone who indulged in curricle races and wore low-cut gowns was a far cry from the very proper Cynthia whom he admired so greatly.

Juliana blushed at the memories of her erratic behaviour. The earl might possibly consider her suitable for someone like Johnny, but never for himself. No, if he ever wed again, it would be with a very proper young lady. Someone like Cynthia, who would not turn his house upside down and embroil him in scandalous escapades.

Tears threatened and Juliana stood up resolutely, tossing the pillow aside. She must tell Georgia of her decision to leave—tell her before her determination wavered and she gave in to the longing to remain near the earl. It was too tempting to stay here where she would occasionally see Granville, where she might have the opportunity to dance with him again or drive out with him. No, she told herself sternly, she must leave. Seeing him would only intensify her feelings and make it more difficult than if she left now. She would return to Anna's and find another position. A position where the work would be hard and she would be too weary at day's end to think about Granville.

Juliana lifted her chin and drew her wrapper round her before marching down the hall to Georgia's room. She tapped softly on the door, almost hoping Georgia had retired, but the maid admitted her at once. Georgia was sitting before her dressing table, her long blond hair brushed out and curling down below her shoulders.

Even from across the room, Georgia could see the distress on Juliana's face, and she nodded dismissal to her maid before rising and crossing to Juliana's side. "What is it, darling? You look as though you have lost your best friend," she said and, with a comforting arm about Juliana's shoulders, drew her to the cream-and-gold sofa.

"I came to thank you for everything you have done and to tell you that I am leaving tomorrow," Juliana murmured, her head down and her hands unconsciously tightening on the older woman's.

"Leaving? Juliana, what nonsense is this?"

"I am sorry, Georgia, but I am going back to Anna's. I have... I have considered it carefully, and I find I cannot marry Johnny, after all. It would not be fair of me to remain here."

Georgia sat back, studying the slender girl beside her. "Are you certain?" she asked, playing for time. It was obvious the child had finally opened her eyes and realized she was in love with Spencer, but why did she wish to leave?

Juliana nodded, swallowing hard. "I have some of the advance on my salary left and I will return that to Lord Granville."

"Do not be foolish, Juliana. Granville will not want your money and it was agreed from the start that you were not constrained to wed Johnny if you found you could not care for him, but I own I am confused. I thought you were fond of my nephew and I know he cares a great deal about you."

Juliana laughed softly even as she blinked back tears. "He cares a great deal about every woman he meets. It is part of his charm."

"Well, yes, but he seemed to be particularly attentive to you. Everyone has remarked on it."

"Johnny treats me as he would a sister—well, not quite that, perhaps. He flirts with me sometimes, but it is more of a habit with him than anything else."

"Marriages have been based on much less and worked successfully, my dear. Unless your heart is engaged elsewhere, you could still wed Johnny and enjoy a life of leisure and if you were unable to feel the more tender emotions, well, you could both go your own way. It is not unheard of in the ton, you know," Georgia said, deliberately prodding her, hoping she would confide her feelings for Spencer.

"I cannot, Georgia. Please do not press me. You do not understand."

"I understand a great deal more than you know, Juliana. You will be giving up a life of wealth and position for one of drudgery. Are you certain you know what you are doing?" she asked. Juliana continued to sit with her head bowed, but her shoulders were shaking and Georgia knew the child was crying silently. She put an arm about the girl, hugging her warmly. "At least take some time to think over your decision. Stay here for another week. What can a few more days signify?"

Juliana rose, shaking her head, barely able to speak. "I cannot." She unfolded a lace handkerchief and wiped at her eyes, swallowing back the sobs which threatened to overwhelm her. When she could speak again, she extended a hand to Georgia. "I must thank you for everything you have done. You have been more than kind and I—"

"I will not allow you to say goodbye," Georgia interrupted, holding her hand tight. "If you insist on leaving, you must at least promise to write to me often and to visit occasionally."

Juliana nodded and impulsively kissed the older woman on the cheek before running from the room.

Georgia watched her go, shaking her head at such folly. It was fortunate her own family and friends had her near at hand to arrange matters. Left to their own devices, they would make sad work of their lives. She rang for her maid and sat down, mentally composing a note for Spencer.

LADY ALYNWICK was not the only one with a desire to meddle in Granville's affairs. While she was busy penning a note for that gentleman, Johnny was being admitted to the house on Cavendish Square by the reluctant butler who had tried, unsuccessfully, to deny his master was at home.

"I will wait, then," Johnny said, divesting himself of his hat and driving coat. "When do you expect him to return?"

Hadley helplessly accepted the garments and stepped back a pace, blocking the hall. "My lord is, that is to say, he is not precisely out."

Johnny looked at him with raised brows.

"Lord Granville is in the library, sir, but he wishes to be left undisturbed. I am ordered not to admit visitors."

"That hardly applies to me, Hadley. In the library, you say? Don't trouble yourself—I know the way, and if Granville objects I shall tell him I knocked you down and stepped over your body."

Hadley moved aside and shrugged. Short of physically restraining him, there was no way to prevent Lord John from entering, and given the younger man's physical attributes, he doubted that even if he dared to lift a hand he would be successful. And there was even the chance, considering Lord Granville's partiality for his brother, that the visit might prove beneficial. Hadley was not one to frown upon a man having a drink or two, but his lordship had been dipping into the brandy rather heavily. The butler lingered in the hall, near the library door, and when Lord John was not immediately ousted, discreetly retired.

Johnny, after one glance inside the room, quietly closed the door behind him and leaned against it, watching his brother. Granville did not appear to have noticed anyone was in the room. He was sprawled in a wing chair near the fireplace, his chin on his chest and one arm dangling over the side of the chair, his fingers holding a brandy glass at a precarious angle.

"Having a private celebration, Spence?"

"What?" Granville lifted his head a fraction and turned bleary eyes in the direction of the door. "Oh, it's you."

"I hope you are not expecting anyone else—not in your condition," Johnny said, sauntering towards him. He drew a matching chair near and seated himself so he could see his brother's face. "I drove Juliana home, if you are interested. Dashed rude of you to leave Almack's without a word to her."

"Knew you'd see her home," Granville replied, waving his glass carelessly. Brandy sloshed onto his shirt and he looked down, surprised.

"I did, though it interfered with certain other arrangements I had made with a new actress at Drury Lane. She's a taking little thing."

"An actress! Damn it, Johnny. Juliana is—she's worth six of any actress," Granville growled, suddenly struggling to sit up.

Johnny grabbed the glass of brandy, what was left of it, and set it on the table. He'd never seen his brother in his cups before and wondered if Spencer was capable of understanding anything he said. Well, all he could do was try. He leaned back in his own chair and made a show of taking out his snuffbox. "The thing is Sally—the actress I was speaking of—thinks I am perfectly wonderful while your Juliana tends to find me merely amusing."

Granville grunted. He was having difficulty focusing his eyes, and there seemed to be two images of Johnny swaying before him. He wished the boy would sit still.

Johnny returned the enamelled box to his pocket and rose. "I was going to offer for her tonight."

"Marry an actress? Have you run mad?" Granville growled, unreasoning anger darkening his eyes. That his brother could wed Juliana and chose instead to dally with an actress infuriated him. He stumbled to his feet, reaching blindly for Johnny. "I will—"

Johnny, with one deft push of his hand, shoved Spencer back into the chair. "I was not referring to the actress," he said loudly, trying to puncture his brother's brandy-induced haze. "Really, Spence, did you have to choose tonight to get foxed?"

Granville stared at him and Johnny couldn't help grinning. "We need to talk, brother of mine, but first I think some coffee. You do not object, do you?" he asked, pulling the bellrope.

Granville didn't answer. He was sitting slumped in the chair, his head in his hands. It is doubtful that he heard the butler arrive, or Johnny giving orders for strong, black coffee. He was, in fact, not aware of anything, until Johnny placed a cup of the steaming hot beverage in front of him. Then he merely stared at it.

"Come on, old fellow, drink up. We need to talk and I cannot do so with you when you're so cup-shot."

Granville shook his head, mumbling, "Old. Too old. Go away, Johnny. Leave me alone."

"Not until you drink some coffee," Johnny said, shaking his head, and putting the cup in Granville's hand. "Don't be stubborn, Spence. I need to talk to you about Juliana."

"Marry her, Johnny," he mumbled, managing a sip of the scalding hot liquid. He drew back with a grimace, but Johnny would not allow it and forced more of the brew down his lips. Granville spluttered and choked and finally threatened to rearrange his brother's features.

Johnny laughed. "That's better. A little more coffee and you might even be able to manage it."

Granville glared, but as Johnny moved towards him again, he lifted the cup and drained it. The room was beginning to lose its blurry edges, but as his vision cleared, his head began to ache alarmingly. He reached up a hand to his brow, the gesture one of excruciating pain.

Johnny refilled his cup, encouraged when Spencer did not object, and waited patiently for his brother to drink it. He listened without comment to irate grumblings which made little sense, and ignored the occasional aspersions cast on his own character. It was not until the third cup of coffee that Spencer began to show some signs of rationality.

Granville pushed the cup aside, demanding irritably, "What are you doing here? I told Hadley I was not to be disturbed."

"Don't blame your butler—Hadley did his best—but I forced my way in, and it's a good thing, too, judging from the looks of you. Whatever possessed you to dip so deep? It's not like you."

"No, that is more your style," Granville replied tartly, with a touch of his old self. "As for what possessed me, that, my dear brother, is not your affair and I very much wish you would go away."

"Not until I have a word with you about Juliana," Johnny said, and was pleased to see Granville was now all attention.

"My mind is a trifle hazy, but did you say you offered for her tonight? If it's my blessing you want, you have it and whatever else you need discuss can surely wait until morning."

"You misunderstood, Spence, which is hardly surprising, given your state of mind. What I said was, I *intended* to offer for Juliana. I know you wish to see me married and setting up a nursery, and I am fond of the girl. In fact, I like her better than any other young woman I've met. If I indeed must settle down with one lady for life, I would as lief it be someone like Juliana who would at least not bore me to tears. There is only one small problem."

"I assume that sooner or later you will get to the point," Granville said, wishing fervently that he had not had quite so much to drink. The pain in his head was abominable.

"The point is, she won't have me."

"Why? What have you done?" he demanded, his pain forgotten as he ruthlessly suppressed the surge of hope he felt.

"Nothing. Even you must admit I have been a pattern card of respectability since we've been in Town. The thing is, she's in love with someone else."

"Impossible! Why, she hasn't shown an ounce of partiality for any other gentleman. There has not been a whisper—"

"Excepting you, Spence," Johnny interrupted quietly.

Granville stared at him. Obviously the brandy had gone to his head and he had not heard his brother correctly.

"I know it sounds implausible, but it seems it's you she wants, though I did my best to cut you out. She won't have me—would not even listen to an offer."

"Nonsense! You cannot be serious. I am too old for Juliana. Everyone has said so."

"Everyone but Juliana," Johnny said, and laughed at the ludicrous expression on his brother's face before adding a warning. "If you mean to have her, you had best act quickly. She is leaving tomorrow."

Granville sat up. "What? Impossible! There is no reason for Juliana to leave, and where would she go? What foolishness is this, Johnny?"

"Word of honour, Spence. Juliana told me herself, though she would not confide in me her reasons. As to where she's going, I believe she mentioned something about her old nurse. Goodwill? Goodboy? Something like that."

"Goodbody," Spencer corrected absently. "But I don't understand why she would leave. She was employed for a year and—"

"Employed? By whom? What are you talking about?" Johnny asked, his brow furrowed in puzzlement.

"Oh, uh, nothing," Granville said, rising and pacing the room. He turned on his brother suddenly. "Look, Johnny, if what you say is true, then you must excuse me. I have to speak with Juliana at once."

Johnny withdrew his pocket watch and glanced at it. "Better have some more coffee, brother. It's close on two in the morning. Juliana will be abed by now."

Granville was out of the room before Johnny had finished speaking, and his younger brother stared after him. Spencer had always been the sober one in the family, the one who looked after him and bailed him out of scrapes. Was that about to change? Was he going to have to start looking after his brother? He shook his head, helping himself to the brandy. Good thing if Spence did marry, he thought. Wouldn't do to have the old fellow in his cups all the time and running around Town in the small hours of the morning. Well, Aunt Georgia would attend to him if he showed up in Grosvenor Square, but Lord, he'd love to see her face.

JOHNNY WOULD NOT have rested so easily had he heard his brother's orders as he rapidly changed his clothes. A sleepy-eyed valet was instructed to send a message to the stables. Granville wanted a horse saddled and brought to the front of the house. Specifically a white stallion. It said much for the respect in which Lord Granville was held that his servants did not question him, and the earl did not choose to enlighten his servants. He mounted the restive stallion in front of the house, swinging the cape of his riding coat behind him and tilting his beaver hat at a rakish angle. The stallion reared on his hind legs, but Granville only laughed and tightened the reins. "Keep a candle burning, Hadley, and expect me when you see me," he called over his shoulder as he set the powerful horse to cantering across the square.

Riding to his aunt's house was an easy matter. There was little traffic at that hour of the morning and a full moon clearly illuminated the streets. An exhilaration he had not felt since he was a boy lightened his spirits and Granville laughed aloud as the stallion danced skittishly round a stray cat. Glancing up at the oval moon, he wondered if it was a touch of moonlight madness compelling him to behave so recklessly. Then he imagined he saw Juliana's face in the moon and laughed again, urging his stallion on: "Hurry up, fellow, for this way lies madness and I am anxious to savour it to the full."

Granville sobered slightly as he approached Grosvenor Square. His aunt's house was darkened and the only sound was a stray dog baying at the moon. He dismounted, leading the nervous stallion along the low railing fronting the block of houses, and slipped through the gate at the end. Granville knew the Square as well as his own house. He and Johnny had played there every summer when they were boys and he recalled his brother scaling an old oak tree at the rear of the house. Its gnarled limbs reached near the upper windows—windows of the room which Juliana was now occupying. He hoped the tree was as sturdy as he remembered.

The huge oak still stood and Granville, looking up at it, wondered briefly if he had lost his mind. The stallion nickered, nudging him with his head, and Granville took it as encouragement and spoke quietly to the horse before tying the reins to a nearby shrub. The night was warm and he removed his driving coat, laying it across the stallion's saddle. His frock coat followed. He would need as much freedom of movement as possible.

Granville gripped a lower limb and pulled himself up, gasping for breath as he straddled the heavy branch. He waited a moment for his heart to steady its beat and then hoisted himself to his feet. He cautiously tested the next branch before grasping the strong limb above his head, and inching upwards. *This isn't so difficult,* he thought, and then clutched wildly at a branch as he narrowly missed his footing. He clung to the tree, doubting his sanity and glanced down longingly to where his stallion waited. Then he froze as he heard a loud voice calling out from the front of the house. All he needed was for the watch to appear and arrest him as a housebreaker.

He waited until the night was silent again to begin climbing once more. The branches were as thick as his thigh and solid even so high up in the tree. Granville, feeling more confident, glanced round to discover Juliana's window nearly opposite. He twisted his body so he was facing the window, his legs straddling the branch. All he needed to do was attract her attention. Juliana would open the window and he could climb in. It should be easy, he thought. Lord knows Johnny had done it often enough.

He edged forward along the limb, stretching his hand to reach a slender branch which nearly brushed the window. If he could manage to scratch it across the panes, surely it would wake Juliana. He strained his body, barely managing to reach the branch, and shook it vigorously. It scraped the window, sounding ominously loud to his ears, but there was no sign of stirring within the house. Granville shook the branch again and waited hopefully. After a moment, he broke off several small twigs and tossed them against the window. That was better, he thought, and repeated the process. A minute later, he saw the flare of a candle as the curtains were drawn aside.

Juliana opened the casement and peered out into the night, but she was looking into the yard below. She gasped, seeing the white stallion tied to the shrub and opened her lips to utter a scream. Only Granville's soft voice urgently whispering her name stayed the sound.

Juliana lifted the candle higher and saw Lord Granville seated on a limb of the gnarled old oak tree and blinked rapidly. Surely she must be dreaming! It could not be the earl perched precariously in a tree and grinning at her like a drunken sot.

"Are you not surprised, Juliana?" the earl whispered, edging forward on the branch which swayed alarmingly. "I must have a word with you and remembered this old tree. It is irregular, of course, but I am not so old after all that I am incapable of—"

"Granville!" she cried as the limb shook and he nearly lost his hold. "Don't move. Can you not see that branch will not support you? Good heavens! Are you mad, sir?"

"Mad? Quite possibly," he owned, clutching the limb more securely. "I thought it would be romantic to vault into your room and propose but I confess I am feeling a trifle light-headed."

Juliana, her large eyes gleaming in the candlelight, gazed at him in astonishment. "I...I beg your pardon? What did you say?"

"I said I am feeling a trifle light-headed," Granville obliged, moving cautiously forward. "But you must not think I am foxed. Johnny poured pots of coffee into me and I—" His words broke off sharply as he lost his grip and suddenly plunged through the leafy branches of the oak.

Juliana screamed and her heart nearly stopped beating as she heard him crashing down through the tree. "Granville? Granville, answer me! Oh, dear God!"

She whirled, her candle flickering, and nearly collided with Georgia just entering the room.

"My dear, whatever is wrong? I thought I heard a scream—"

"It's Granville—he fell from the oak tree," she said, brushing past her and leaving Georgia to stare after her. Juliana rushed down the hall to the back stairs leading to the kitchen, and flew down the steps with little regard for her own safety. The old kitchen was brightly lit and the wide door which led to the vegetable garden stood open. Even as she crossed the room, she could hear raised voices from the yard.

Juliana barely paused as she took in the moonlit scene. Granville lay sprawled on the ground, his head and shoulders supported by one of Georgia's footmen while Grim and two other servants stood over him arguing with an obese individual whose heavy blue coat marked him as a watchman.

"What I should like to know is what the gentleman was doing in the tree if he weren't planning on housebreaking."

"As the gentleman is related to Lady Alynwick, the matter is none of your concern and you may be on your way," Grim said, trying to edge the garrulous watchman towards the gate.

Juliana paid them little heed, pushing aside one of the footmen to kneel at Granville's side. She took his hand in hers and knew a measure of vast relief as he shook his head groggily and opened his eyes. He stared at her for a long moment and she feared he did not recognize her. Then he smiled, a lopsided, quizzical smile.

"What light through yonder window breaks? It is the east and Juliana is the sun," he murmured.

"There, you see," the watchman crowed, tearing his eyes away from Juliana's enticing figure. "Talking about breaking windows he is, and if that don't show he meant to climb in that window up there, I don't know what does."

"You, sir, are a dolt," Georgia said, emerging from the house in time to hear the exchange. "And if you were not so abysmally ignorant you would know my nephew was quoting a line from Shakespeare." She gave him no chance to reply, but turned to Grim. "Escort this man from the premises and if he is at all troublesome, obtain his name and I shall speak to the Home Secretary about him tomorrow."

The watchman cowered before her and meekly allowed Grim to lead him to the gate. His obsequious voice floated back to them. "I was only trying to protect her ladyship..."

Georgia's face softened as she turned and glanced down at her nephew. His shirt was torn, his cravat a hopeless tangle, and he was bleeding from various cuts and scratches. He had never looked more endearing. "Well, Spencer? It appears you have managed to eclipse even Johnny's most foolhardy escapades."

The soft rebuke did not trouble him, and he smiled crookedly up at her. "I meant to, you know."

She shook her head at his nonsense but her voice was gentle. "I shall not trouble you for an explanation at present, but pray tell me if you are able to stand. If not, the footmen will carry you into the house."

Granville tentatively moved one booted foot and bit his lip as a sharp pain shot up his leg. He tried but was not quite able to mask the agony in his eyes though he managed a smile. "An ignoble end to a daring deed. I fear they must carry me."

IT WAS NEARLY DAWN before Juliana was able to speak with Granville alone. The doctor, who had tended both Spencer and Johnny when they were younger, had not wasted his breath on foolish questions. He excluded the ladies from the room while he examined Granville and then told them over coffee that apparently the lower limbs of the tree had lessened the impact of Granville's fall. He had numerous cuts and scratches, and his right leg, though bruised and swollen, did not appear to be broken. But, he had added ominously, his lordship had severely twisted the leg and it would be three weeks or more before it could bear his weight again.

Lord Granville had taken the news stoically, but was restive, and Grim reported that he was asking for Miss Chevron.

Juliana looked at the kindly doctor questioningly.

"If you don't mind, miss, it would be well to have a word with him. Best if he's kept quiet."

Juliana was gone before anyone else could object, but she paused outside the drawing-room door, trying to collect her thoughts. For the past two hours she had agonized over Granville's actions and his words, trying to puzzle out his intentions. Neither she nor Georgia had been able to conceive of what insane impulse had compelled Granville to attempt to climb the old oak. And Juliana had not mentioned his strange proposal just before he'd fallen. She was not entirely certain that she had not imagined the words he had uttered and was almost afraid to hope he had meant them.

She tapped softly on the door and opened it slowly. Granville lay stretched out on the crimson sofa, his right leg shorn of his boot and elevated on pillows. His face was paler than usual, but his blue eyes had an amused look and he smiled warmly when he saw her.

Juliana fought the urge to run to his side and hold him in her arms. He looked a far cry from the haughty, well-dressed earl she was accustomed to seeing. She walked across the room, deliberately measuring her steps, until she was a few feet from him.

"My dear, do not be frightened," he said, seeing the nervous way her hands pleated the handkerchief she held. "Did I give you a scare?"

She nodded shyly. "At first I thought a burglar was outside, and then, when I realized it was you, I felt I must be dreaming. But I wasn't truly frightened—that is, not until you fell."

Granville looked away, his voice full of self-loathing. "In the future I shall leave such feats to Johnny. He would have carried it off in style instead of tumbling from the tree like some clumsy oaf."

Juliana drew nearer, kneeling beside the sofa. "I doubt Johnny would have ever tried anything so daring, and I know he would not be capable of quoting Shakespeare if ever he did."

Granville turned his head, and Juliana saw the tiny scratch which ran down his jaw, from just below his eye to the corner of his lips. She tightened her hands to keep from reaching out and touching it.

"You must think me an idiot," Granville said, his eyes intent on hers.

"No, never that," she answered a trifle breathlessly.

"I had some notion, you see, that you might think it admirable if I rode here on a white stallion, climbed the tree, vaulted into your room and . . . proposed."

Juliana's smile lit her face as though the sun had suddenly risen. Her eyes sparkled like the morning dew, nudging her lips to open slightly like a budding rose. The joy shining from her eyes was blinding, but he did not look away and it was she who lowered her lashes. "Admirable, but hardly necessary. A conventional proposal would have been just as acceptable."

"Juliana," he said, catching her hand up in his. "Do you truly mean that? You don't think I am too old for you?"

"I think, dear sir, that you are perfect in every way..." she said, her words a mere whisper fading into the train of her thoughts as she felt his hand in her hair, drawing her head down to his. She met his lips willingly and with a passion she had not known she possessed. When he released her, she touched the scratch on his cheek with her lips, trailing kisses upwards to his eye.

Granville groaned and she sat back alarmed but was instantly reassured by his teasing smile.

"Kiss me like that again, my dear, and you will likely find that I am not a very proper gentleman at all," he said, his hand fingering the folds of her dressing gown where they lay against her throat.

"I fear I do not care much for propriety," she said, and would have dared to kiss him again had not Georgia sailed imperiously into the room.

"Well, darlings, is it all settled?" she asked, smiling fondly at them both.

Spencer looked at her, his brows raised. "Is what settled, Aunt?"

"Your betrothal, of course, and I must say it has taken you long enough to come to the point. Now do behave, Spencer, we have a great deal to plan. I thought December for your wedding—''

"September," he said firmly.

"Darling, that is only a month away. Why, it is hardly time enough to assemble Juliana's bridal clothes."

"The first of September," he repeated, one arm holding Juliana firmly to his side, while she smiled tenderly down at him.

"Spencer, you are not thinking clearly. No doubt it was the fall. Why, whatever would people say?"

"Probably that the very proper Lord Granville has taken leave of his senses, but I find I do not care what anyone else thinks. You have until September, my dearest Aunt, and not a day more. I suggest you start on the arrangements at once, and would you be good enough to close the door on your way out?"

Georgia obliged him, astonished at the change in her elder nephew. She shut the door softly, a small smile on her lips. It was wonderful having the old Spencer back again, she thought, and was still lingering in the hall when Johnny entered a few moments later.

"I was on my way to my rooms when I saw all the lights. I gather Spence paid you a call."

"A most spectacular one," she agreed, laughing. "You might say he dropped in on us."

"Out with it, Madam Aunt. What mischief are you brewing? You have the look of the devil in your eyes."

"You do me an injustice, my dear," she said, hooking her arm in his. "I was merely thinking of your brother's betrothal."

"Ah, is it settled, then? But what is so amusing? I thought Juliana would have your blessing."

"Oh, she does, darling. She does," she said, looking up fondly at him, her lips curved in a wicked smile. "But I was just thinking that *dear Cynthia* would not approve of this, no, she wouldn't approve of this marriage at all."

The two madcaps strolled down the hall, their soft laughter echoing in their wake.

Harlequin Regency Romance ™

COMING NEXT MONTH

#77 WAYWARD ANGEL by Vivian Keith
Miss Annabelle Winthrop recognized her feelings for
Camford Singletary, the Earl of Westerbrook,
immediately. Yet he struggled to resist similar
feelings for her. Annabelle committed herself to
teaching him that it was better to have loved and lost
than never to have loved at all.

#78 BITTERSWEET REVENGE by Gail Whitiker
Miss Regana Kently had no reason to hope that she
of all ladies would attach the interest of the
"Unmarriageable Earl" of Westmorlen. And even
less expectations that he would ask her to become his
countess. Nevertheless, she was devastated to learn
of the earl's devilish scheme to marry her and kill
two birds with one stone.

Take 4 bestselling love stories FREE
Plus get a FREE surprise gift!

FREE GIFT OFFER

To receive your free gift, send us the specified number of proofs-of-purchase from any specially marked Free Gift Offer Harlequin or Silhouette book with the Free Gift Certificate properly completed, plus a check or money order (do not send cash) to cover postage and handling payable to Harlequin/Silhouette Free Gift Promotion Offer. We will send you the specified gift.

FREE GIFT CERTIFICATE

ITEM	A. GOLD TONE EARRINGS	B. GOLD TONE BRACELET	C. GOLD TONE NECKLACE
# of proofs-of-purchase required	3	6	9
Postage and Handling	$1.75	$2.25	$2.75
Check one	☐	☐	☐

Name: _____

Address: _____

City: _____ State: _____ Zip Code: _____

Mail this certificate, specified number of proofs-of-purchase and a check or money order for postage and handling to: HARLEQUIN/SILHOUETTE FREE GIFT OFFER 1992, P.O. Box 9057, Buffalo, NY 14269-9057. Requests must be received by July 31, 1992.

PLUS—Every time you submit a completed certificate with the correct number of proofs-of-purchase, you are automatically entered in our MILLION DOLLAR SWEEPSTAKES! No purchase or obligation necessary to enter. See below for alternate means of entry and how to obtain complete sweepstakes rules.

MILLION DOLLAR SWEEPSTAKES
NO PURCHASE OR OBLIGATION NECESSARY TO ENTER

To enter, hand-print (mechanical reproductions are not acceptable) your name and address on a 3" ×5" card and mail to Million Dollar Sweepstakes 6097, c/o either P.O. Box 9056, Buffalo, NY 14269-9056 or P.O. Box 621, Fort Erie, Ontario L2A 5X3. Limit: one entry per envelope. Entries must be sent via 1st-class mail. For eligibility, entries must be received no later than March 31, 1994. No liability is assumed for printing errors, lost, late or misdirected entries.

Sweepstakes is open to persons 18 years of age or older. All applicable laws and regulations apply. Sweepstakes offer void wherever prohibited by law. Prizewinners will be determined no later than May 1994. Chances of winning are determined by the number of entries distributed and received. For a copy of the Official Rules governing this sweepstakes offer, send a self-addressed, stamped envelope (WA residents need not affix return postage) to: Million Dollar Sweepstakes Rules, P.O. Box 4733, Blair, NE 68009.

HG3U

ONE PROOF-OF-PURCHASE
To collect your fabulous FREE GIFT you must include the necessary FREE GIFT proofs-of-purchase with a properly completed offer certificate.

(See inside back cover for offer details)